Faith

or

Fiction

PAM DUNN

A catalogue record for this book is available from the National Library of Australia

Publisher: **Inspiring Publishers,**
P.O. Box 159, Calwell, ACT Australia 2905
Email: publishaspg@gmail.com
http://www.inspiringpublishers.com

National Library of Australia The Prepublication Data Service

Author: Dunn, Pam

Title: **Faith or Fiction/**_Pam Dunn_

ISBN: 978-1-922618-15-3 (Print)
        978-1-922618-16-0 (eBook)

Bibliography: Scripture quotations are from The Good News Translation

Revised Edition - © American Bible Society 1966, 1971, 1976, 1992 with Deuterocanonicals/Apocrypha.

SUMMARY

Many years ago it started, and just like today when I sit down to write, many things enter my mind and today is no exception. I especially await the voice that so gently enters in at certain times - a voice I am well familiar with as I have heard it many times before. It never alarms me in any way for it brings with it much peace and wisdom. Today that voice has given me the following words and in obedience to that voice, I write them here to intro·duce this book.

Words Received:

"People must understand that as you write this book there will be times in it when the words you write will be given by the voice. If they believe it - it will be by faith - if they do not believe that you hear them and write them, then let them believe they are fiction.

It was some twenty four years ago that the covering was removed and you remember clearly that day also as you sat and felt the whirlwind start at your feet and continue on up encircling your body as it did until it exited from the top of your head. You remember how you sat there quietly reflecting on what had happened – for you knew that the dome, the covering had just been removed. You even told yourself, 'I am just me now'. That Pam is why that old movie has remained in your mind and why it has been kept until this time to have it recalled. You see, it foreshadowed your own life. The day the covering was removed you were made open to all the elements of the world with every devil able to approach you. And approach you they did, disguised as lights and some wearing shining armour."

INTRODUCTION

Many years ago as a young teenage girl, I viewed a movie in which a young novice in an order of nuns was enticed by the devil to leave her nunnery and pursue a life with a young soldier who was passing through that town.

After this, no one missed the young novice from their midst as the statue in the church where they prayed went missing at the same time. No one connected the statues disappearance with the young novice as far as they were concerned, she was still with them. In other words the statue had become her and filled in for the young novice.

As the story continued us the audience found how hard it became for that part of the country and surrounding villages, lack of rain, crops withering in the fields with dust storms and much heat for the people to cope with, the people were faced with much misery.

Even though the nuns and the priests along with the villages all continued on the best they could to remain faithful to their faith and trust in God, things just seemed to continue on becoming even more desperate.

As a young girl I remember watching the dust and the heat whirling around the large screen as the poor animals tried to survive the elements that were facing them and the poor people of the village whose energy also appeared to be slipping away from them.

Then just at this point in the movie – which I must explain was right towards the end – one morning as they entered the church they found the statue back on its stand as if by a miracle and their joy was great at seeing this.

Unbeknown to any, that same night the young novice had given away her new life style with the young soldier and had returned to the convent to resume her place.

We were led to believe that the statue had changed itself into the young novice to take her place so no one would find her missing. The statue in the story was that of the Blessed Virgin Mary the Holy Mother of God, who protected her daughter the novice, allowing her to return to God and serve him according to her first desire. Satan had been defeated by the Holy Mother of Jesus and one of her many children had been snatched back from his hands.

I recall this movie vividly and over the years have pondered about it on many occasions, thinking when we are not in the place that God wants us to be or not doing what he wants, how much harder life becomes for us and those around us, for the blessings and graces appear to become fewer and fewer and in many cases life becomes harder and harder as if God is trying to give us a wakeup call to check just where we are in our relationship with him.

Hopefully, this is when we come to our senses and with humility take a good look at our lives to see if we are somewhere we should not be. Just maybe we are being held with our heads just above water and close to drowning if it was not for some kind souls praying to the Virgin Mary for our protection.

I have called this manuscript Faith or Fiction - for those who read it with faith will I hope, know where I am coming from, and those who will read it as fiction, will come to see their world of fiction with new eyes.

Maybe it would be better to say the opposite side of the same coin of life. One side of the coin we see faith on the other side we see fiction, but both so closely connected.

1
TRUE DEVOTION TO MARY

Over the last few weeks I have come across an old book of mine, it was a book I had been advised by a priest to read many years ago and as I flipped through the pages, I found I had written down in the margin in pencil the following words.

'Today is the 14th June 2001 – this spoke to my heart. May God have mercy on me, Amen'

The little book was called; 'True Devotion to Mary' and it had been written by St. Louis De Montfort and translated by Father Frederick Faber. The particular chapter in this book that had caused my mind to venture into what I am writing came from what in the book is called the 'Fifth Truth' – that is, we need Mary in order to preserve the grace and treasures we have received from God.

As I continue on, I am told that this work by St Louis de Montfort was written in a time when Jansenism, which opposed devotion to the Blessed Virgin, was flourishing throughout Europe. Even eminent authors were deceived by this heretical sect.

Today I know that there are many who have turned their back upon the Blessed Mother and anything resembling a devotion of any kind to her. I wonder if we have allowed the devils who are skillful thieves, to strip us of the one who can crush the head of these miserable critters who watch day and night for a favorable moment to deceive us and snatch the grace that we have been given away from us in a moment by a sin, where all our graces and merits that we have gained for many years are lost.

Oh, we should be so afraid of their evil tricks that they play especially as they turn them into things that look so appealing.

As you may have guessed the one who is writing these words is no longer young, but a woman in her seventies, so I feel free to share my journey and the experiences of my walk with God and His Blessed Mother.

Again I ask that anyone who may read what is written here will accept it as true faith for that is what it is. If anyone is unable to accept it as truth, then I hope you will continue on reading even if you can only accept it as fiction. Although it is not fiction, for it is too late in my life to say it is in order to make up a good story. For I know not when I will have to kneel before the one I claim to have heard all from and therefore all I proclaim here is truth.

A Child of Mary

I was about fourteen years old when I was made a Child of Mary and it was at the dedication night to our Blessed Mother that I received my first supernatural experience. I was standing in line with other girls who like me were being received into the society of The Children of Mary. We had our Blue Cloaks around us and wore white veils. As the line progressed I could see each girl in front of me take her position in front of the priest where she made her commitment to Our Lady. I was about third in line now, when I felt such a wonderful feeling come upon me. It was as if someone had covered me with a dome. Just like the ones with the snowflakes inside them that you see at Christmas time. It felt like everything became silent and the peace was amazing. I just wanted to stand there and not move. After sometime I realized the line was about to move and I felt if I did not move forward, someone would have to encourage me from behind to do so.

One of my friends in the line passed away this year and it would have been roughly fifty five years ago from that night when we had stood in the line and made our vows as Children of Mary. My friend had remained in our home town all her life and was greatly appreciated by the community by the number of people who were there attending her funeral in the very same church we had made our vows to be Children of Mary so long ago. As I gazed upon the photos contained in the memorial booklet given to us at our attendance I came upon a photo of my friend standing with her mother and her sister and there she stood proudly wearing her blue cloak and white veil. She had remained faithful to her vow to Our Lady as her rosary beads were very prevalent at her funeral.

May she rest in peace and a perpetual light shine upon her, Amen.

Covering Dome Removed

Much has happened since the day the dome was placed upon me in that line - many wonderful things spiritually, and many not so wonderful things, in regard to sickness. It seemed to follow me like a plague - nothing ever the same, something new and unusual every time. It took a toll upon my person and my family and looking back I realise just how close I came to losing my life a number of times - I acknowledge the intercession of our Blessed Lady as the night I knew I was dying and I called out to her, "Holy Mother of God please help me". I was suffering from a rupture lining of my diaphragm which allowed my stomach to push my heart and lung to one side and this led to the doctors believing I had a cyst on my right lung. On seeking specialist advice, I was told if it had not stopped where it did I would be on a slab in the morgue now. I have always believed that night when I called out in fear and pain to Our Lady, she had intervened for my life. That was in the early seventies, and I believe it was when Our Lady truly began to intercede for me, for I felt the devil tried so many times to take my life from me. But God in His mercy allowed me to receive medical help to help me survive.

Although it would be very unfair if I did not tell you about how God himself touched me when I was to be sent to professional doctors in Sydney to have my leg stiffened. I had been suffering from a ruptured Achilles tendon for over five years. It had been operated on twice to try and rejoin it without success. On the second try I had been placed in plaster from my toes to my knee for six months and on crutches to get around - while trying to look after my four young children proved to be frustrating at times. But this was the last try and now all they could see at the time to help me was to stiffen my leg so I would have something secure to walk on.

Six weeks before I was to go to Sydney for this procedure, I had by God's grace, through our prayer group, been invited to attend a charismatic healing gathering in our town.

I did attend with great joy in my heart to hear that Our Lord Jesus Christ was using people in his ministry to heal just as he had foretold in Holy Scripture.

That night I was asked to sit upon an old wooden chair and the servant of God asked me if I believed God could heal me? I replied, "Yes I believe God can heal, but I don't know if he would want to heal me or not". That was how I felt; I believed He could heal anyone there in the room, but I was just me and that was where the doubt lay. I was no one.

As I finished writing the above – I began to receive the following words;

You were one child, with no hope of moving forward without great help. As you finished your last sentence you said you were nobody. It was in that thought that you became even closer to God and me than you could imagine. You had no thought about the many gifts that were to fall upon your life. And as each one did, you began to grow and grow and like a strong tree you stood tall among my children in your knowledge and love for me and my beloved son.

Then as time moved on and many people desired to hear about what was happening in your life and in many more cases in theirs, by the words that would flow effortlessly from your lips placed there by the God you serve. You gave and you gave, and they came and they took all that you had been given and embellished it with their own thoughts which enabled it to lose much of the anointing.

Pam, I say anointing for they were anointed words and you gave them as such. Under the anointing, the words became powerful and those who heard them and believed were greatly touched.

It was some twenty four years ago that the covering was removed and you remember clearly that day also as you sat and felt the whirlwind start at your feet and continue on up encircling your body as it did until it exited from the top of your head. You remember how you sat there quietly reflecting on what had happened - for you knew that the dome, the covering had just been removed. You even told yourself, 'I am just me now'. That Pam is why that old movie has remained in your mind and why it has been kept until this time to have it recalled. You see, it foreshadowed your own life. The day the covering was removed you were made open to all the elements of the world with every devil able to approach you. And approach you they did, disguised as lights and some wearing shining armor.

Others, who truly had believed in all that could be seen as truly coming from God, wanted so much to help and some by their helping only began to interfere and soon the enemy had made an opening among my children who had fallen to his wicked scheme. You too began to wonder who to trust and in this way Satan was able to shut you down and cause you to remain hidden from sight. Like the girl in the old movie you were there but not known. Some twenty four years later I have come to bring you back to your rightful place among my people.

I have continued to encourage many to pray for you so that the enemy will not overpower you with his lies and deception. I want you to write all that you know in your heart as truth coming from the Holy One who has been with you always. The Spirit of God, so lovingly given and who remains within all hearts that are open to him, he will bring that soul into a safe harbour after it has travelled the treacherous waters and weathered the storms that raged against it in its times of testing, without the covering protection of God and his Blessed Mother.

People must understand that as you write this book there will be times in it when the words you write will be given by another voice and if they believe it - it will be by faith- if they do not believe that you hear them and write them let them then believe they are fiction.

This I ask of you, do not be afraid to write what you hear and place the words just as you hear them upon the page. Do not be anxious of what others may say or think for you know the truth, in faith, what they mean.

Before you were born you were marked to bring these words to the world you live in today. It is a far different world than the one my servant St Louis de Montfort lived in. But the challenges are much the same in the spiritual world. Demons still roam the earth looking to cause as much mischief as they can. They have invaded weak minds of the enemies of Christ to spread lies and deception using any kind of media they can to invade the thoughts, the homes and minds of many people, until so much of what today's world calls fake news has been peddled long and hard enough to cause doubts in the hearts and minds of many.

The young who are just finding their voice are crying out the loudest about many things - but many of the things they wish to change in their world is only being exploited by the greedy, the deceitful, and those whose only desire in this world is to make money and to make it any way they can.

There are others whose only motive is to change the world according to what they believe. While others will argue with you about every truth in Holy Scripture until they have almost rewritten the Holy Word according to their belief.

Do not be open to these kinds of people for they will only rob you of your peace and faith. Tell them with love that you respect them to have a view, but that view is not yours and so let the conversation end with neither causing the other to sin by arguing.

This millennium will bring about many changes for the world and the people in it. If I were to tell you – you would die of grief for the findings.

Pam, put on your faith and tightly tie it around your waist for the time is coming when the underlying tension against myself the Mother of the Lord Jesus will raise its ugly head and those who follow my son under the same banner as yourself - will try and make much trouble for you and my priests. I tell you solemnly that you will be protected as you walk under the protection of the Fifth Truth.

I then earnestly prayed 'Oh Mother Mary, we need you in order to protect the graces and treasures we have received from God.'

2.

THE NIGHT MY LEG WAS HEALED

My Prayer

Lord the night you healed my leg your servant who prayed for me, gave me the following words;

"He wants you in His ministry – with women – women who would not normally hear".

I asked the Lord, 'How do I do this Lord? Or is it too late? Has it already been done by others while I was sleeping in the cave'?

Words Received

You were never in the cave Pam, you thought you were but others were making full use of the gift I had given to you. You remained untouched by the public because it was my will, not yours. Child many have tried to follow in emulating your gift, but since you became aware of their actions they can no longer deceive you or others. Bring home those who have followed blindly the one that stole all. Go now, they no longer have a place in your life; your life comes directly under my control. Do not be put off about what you will write, it will just come naturally and the words will flow like silk or honey from the comb.

Pam you are about to wake and take up your position in my army. Go in peace and be encouraged by what I show you. Read Jeremiah Chapter 12: my love for you is great and it will be made known to many soon.

Thank you, Father Son and Holy Spirit.

Amen.

Jeremiah Questions The Lord

12:1-6 'Lord, if I argued my case with you, you would prove to be right. Yet I must question you about matters of justice. Why are the wicked so prosperous?

Why do dishonest people succeed?

You plant them, and they take root; they grow and bear fruit. They always speak well of you, yet they do not really care about you.

But, Lord, you know me; you see what I do and how I love you. Drag these evil people away like sheep to be slaughtered; guard them until it is time for them to be killed.

How long will our land be dry, and the grass in the whole countryside be withered? Animals and birds are dying because of the wickedness of our people, people who say, 'God doesn't see what we are doing.'

The Lord said,

'Jeremiah, if you get tired racing against people, how can you race against horses? If you can't even stand up in open country, how will you manage in the jungle by the Jordan?

Even your relatives, members of your own family, have betrayed you; they join in the attacks against you. Do not trust them, even though they speak friendly words.'

After reading Jerimiah, I continued reading -

The Lord's Sorrow Because of His People -

v7-13 The Lord says,

'I have abandoned Israel; I have rejected my chosen nation. I have given the people I love into the power of their enemies. My chosen people have turned against me; like a lion in the forest they have roared at me, and so I hate them. My chosen people are like a bird attacked from all sides by hawks. Call the wild animals to come and join in the feast! Many foreign rulers have destroyed my vineyard; they have trampled down my crops; they have turned my lovely land into a desert. They have made it a wasteland; it lies desolate before me. The whole land has become a desert, and no one cares. Across all the desert highlands people have come to plunder. I have sent war to destroy the entire land; no one can live in peace. My people planted wheat, but gathered weeds; they have worked hard, but got nothing for it. Because of my fierce anger their crops have failed.'

v 14-17 The Lord's Promise to Israel's Neighbours

The Lord says, 'I have something to say about Israel's neighbours who have ruined the land I gave to my people Israel. I will take those wicked people away from their countries like an uprooted plant, and I will rescue Judah from them. But after I have taken them away, I will have mercy on them; I will bring each nation back to its own land and to its own country. If with all their hearts they will accept the religion of my people and will swear, 'As the Lord lives' – as they once taught my people to swear by Baal – then they will also be a part of my people and will prosper. But if any nation will not obey, then I will completely uproot it and destroy it. I, the Lord, have spoken.'

3.

A NEW DAY

My Prayer

Good morning Lord, I hope today I might be able to get further along with the book. You told me I would receive the words and I was wondering if today that might happen. I know my mind is not in a very friendly place at the moment so if you don't want me to hear anything I will understand.

Words Received

Time stands still for no one Pam, even people like you who desire to listen and write but on many occasions you find your mind wondering into areas that make your will unclean. Don't allow negative thoughts about others put you off, I can overcome that - all I need is for you to take up the pen and then we can begin.

Why do so many people believe that the world will end with a big bang - have I told you that Pam?

No Father, I don't think so.

Then don't let anyone control your thoughts in this regard. The morning has broken and many people including you have thought about what their actions for this day should be. If you are willing to listen, I will tell you something about this new life that has come into people's speech.

Shine forth the wisdom of your God by writing these simple truths upon the page, Holy is My Name and Holy all people must become. Before the devil is let loose to start his bombardment of so many places where people have gathered thinking they are safe. You have just read Jeremiah and you seen what I told him and I tell all my children who desire to listen that things will become tiring for many as the drought drags on and the work force becomes tired.

Show mercy where possible child for there are days coming when many people will begin to lose heart. This is the time I want each of my people to stand tall and tell the children of the earth that they have a great chance to lift their spirits and their hearts to their God of Heaven and earth and watch how when people really walk according to my will, just how the things in the spiritual world will have no power over them. Put away your own way of thinking my people and turn to me to fix the messes of your lives and countries.

My Prayer

Come Holy Spirit, please come, I am so in need of your aid.

Words Received

The wind that howled and the snow that fell will be of little comfort for those who gazed upon its beauty Pam. The animals that shivered and froze in the snow will only long to feel the warm sun upon their skin once more. All things, people, plants, and animals, all have to shiver sometime in their lives otherwise there would be no appreciation of the summer sun.

Daughter, allow me to show you what I want of you. There was a time when my words were always ready to fall upon your mind and today is no different. You will receive them and there will be many. Show the angel that guards you that you are ready to receive all that you hear. Many have waited to bring about the new beginning and there is no time to waste. Finish your book; you will find enough material once you start, so don't be alarmed. Many already have gone on to write a new chapter for themselves, but you have been waiting; don't wait any longer, start this day and remember always, I am with you until the end of time.

My Prayer

Yesterday was a terrible day Lord, but even though I thank you for it. I had no idea about the website that you showed me yesterday. I learned a lot from it. It kind of made me very angry, sad, and a lot of other emotions thrown in at the same time. But today, I have tried to put it all behind me along with the above thoughts and I want to move forward this time as me and not some invisible person.

So here goes Father God, I hope this will be the start of a new day writing for the book.

Mothers and Toddlers; A long time ago you told me at a prayer meeting in Goulburn that we, the older mothers, would be needed to show the young women how to be mothers. I believe that message may have been adopted by others after I had left there. Yet today, I see some mothers unable to control their little children, it seems the children appear to be controlling them, the mothers.

I was told only today that mothers today are not raising children, they are raising adults. Thinking on this I believe that is right. I have witnessed mothers spending so much time on trying to reason with a toddler about many things, even what sweet treats they desire – while oblivious to the fact that they have just blocked an entire lane of a shop for ten minutes or more while they discuss the purchase with a toddler.

I have attended Mass where young children are allowed to run around the church during the service, yelling loudly, while the parent sits quietly unmindful to the distraction it causes to others there.

I have been uncharitable in my thoughts towards such people and wonder why they did not explain to the child that this was Gods house where the people had come to pray and talk to God – and it was not like the park where children were encouraged to run and play and where such actions are acceptable. Everyone knows and accepts certain reactions from children in certain circumstances and will just overlook it – but these days there does not seem to be any discipline for a child to understand that their action is not acceptable to all, in certain places.

4.
I TRY TO FORGIVE

My Prayer

Today is a day of reflection for Me Lord. I know there is much in my heart that I need to let go of – but it is getting harder to do so each day. This morning I heard one of your servants say on the television that when we have been hurt and although we try and forgive and continue to love, we know that we fall short of that Divine Love that only you God has. I do try, but as time goes on and I see others getting away with the acts that have caused one so much pain, anxiety and sorrow. You start to shut down and say even if it be only inwardly, that it was not fair in what you had been made to live through.

But this morning something was said, in fact I was shown two things that really resonated with me. I had risen early to prepare to go to Mass, as it was still very early and there was a Mass being said on the television for those at home, I joined in to participate. It was during the elevation of the

Eucharist that I received a very deep feeling within me as I heard the words spoken by the priest - "do this in memory of me". Here, I was aware of the suffering of the Lord, his body so tortured and beaten. I felt myself saying, oh, it's all about Jesus, it would not have mattered who was beside me or around me at that moment, it was my heart, mind, soul and spirit being connected with this suffering figure that in my mind's eye I could see so clearly.

In that second I knew that this person, this suffering savior was the one I wanted to remember and communicate with. Thanking Him and remembering just what it had taken on his behalf to break the chains of sin and open the gates of heaven to us sinners. And what was he asking? - 'just that when we receive his precious body and blood that we did it remembering just what he had suffered for our freedom.'

Later at morning Mass as I approached the altar to receive that precious body and blood, I remembered other words which he had spoken. (Jn 6:53) "Unless you eat my flesh and drink my blood, you will not have life within you."

Coming back to the other thing I had pondered on this morning being able to forgive others as God forgives me. Yes, it is very hard to forgive and love others after you have been hurt badly, but then I remembered the words of Jesus as he was dying on the cross, He said, (Lk 23:6) "Father forgive them, they know not what they do." With this thought in mind I also asked the Father to forgive all those who had hurt me, for when the pain is so raw and the hurting so bad,

I know, I must still forgive, and this I try and do. So if Jesus asked the Father to forgive them - then anything lacking in my forgiveness for those who had hurt me would be forgiven by my surrendering my hurt to the Father asking in Jesus name for this mercy to help me truly forgive all as I should.

I am not sure if these are the right words to use to try and explain this, but with God's grace and mercy upon my life maybe I too will be able to make sure that even though I may not be able to forget what had happened, I could now hold no resentment or anger towards anyone and healing and mercy towards all would be felt in my own heart. This kind of healing can only come about by the grace of God, Amen.

Words Received

The healing power of my mercy is on its way for you Pam. You have been obedient even when you did not know it. I allowed you to wander into areas you on your own would not have gone, but in doing so you uncovered many things that you would not have known existed.

Believe child in all that I allow to happen and it will all be exposed in the end. Even those that have no faith are beginning to wonder how you are able to come across so much material, especially those they thought they had cleverly concealed.

Open my Holy Word and rejoice in my love for you and all my people.

5.

MY PRAYER TO THE TRINITY

My Prayer

Holy One, Holy Immortal One, Holy God of the Trinity. The Father is God. The Son is God. The Holy Spirit is God. There are three persons – but only one God.

Father, I am not sure if you would ever anoint me again, but even if you don't, I surrender my life into your hands and say you alone are my God, to you alone do I bow. I renounce Satan and all his works. I accept Jesus Christ as my only savior by his sacrifice on the cross and Him alone do I call master.

The Holy Spirit has been the most wonderful gift I have ever received and to God the Holy Spirit the third person of the Blessed Trinity I say; Thank you Holy Spirit for all that you have shown me, and helped me with and for always being there for me, even when I have wandered away from guidance by not listening and writing as often as I should have.

I pray to God the Father and the Son for the grace never to offend you Holy Spirit again. If today I hear your voice, help me not to harden my heart.

Words Received

The dying has been completed my daughter. Angels and saints have already been sent forth into many lands. They are there to gather the remnant of my Holy House and to bring them together. Holy is my name and holy my people must become. Are you ready to begin the work I have called you to do?

Yes Lord, I need you to show me what that work is though?

Pam, before you were born it had been the destiny for your life, to be the person that you are in order to fulfill my will upon the earth at this time. Gently allow me to awaken all that you hold dear in your heart. I desire for you to experience all the joy and peace that you know I am able to give. I am anointing you afresh with new words and with new power to confront the enemy. Before you were born an angel of great strength was sent to guard you. Many times the enemy has tried to eliminate you from this world, but each time my angel defended you. You did not see him or even know that he was beside you. Together now you will understand that he has been with you, and is even at this moment helping you to listen and write.

Be open to the prompting of my Holy Spirit for it is He who will allow you to do the work I am asking of you.

Open your computer now and look for that one that has caused you all the harm, today you will see them clearly.

Child, go in my peace and hold onto my words for they are life for you. Go in peace.

Yesterday, I asked the Lord to show me the work he wanted me to do, so, as I travelled to Mass this morning I began a conversation with my Lord, asking Him how or even what it was I was being asked to do. As I had no idea what it could be. All I knew is that for quite some time I had been hearing the following words;

You have fulfilled the will of the Father - now fulfill the will of the Son.

Arriving at the Church and standing still at the back of the Church, I acknowledged my Lords presence in the tabernacle. And again made the request that I was here Lord, still not knowing what it was I had the feeling I was being called on to do.

It was during the Mass, as the homily was being preached a number of words were spoken that touched me greatly. In the gospel reflection we were asked to remember how last week in the scriptures we were told how Saint Peter had been the only one to identify Jesus as the Christ – the Son of God. And in today's readings Jesus rebukes Peter in the harshest of words that Jesus said to anyone – when he said, *'get behind me Satan'.* (Mt 16:23) Jesus had called Peter the enemy by referring to him as Satan – as Satan is the enemy.

In one week Peter is the one to stop thinking spiritually and begin to think by human reasoning. In thinking spiritually, Peter had been given insight from the Father in heaven to recognize Jesus as the Christ - the Son of God. What a blessing to be given such revelation and I guess many people have been given moments of grace and wisdom from above to receive such insights to know just who Jesus really was and is.

How quickly we can let those moments of great grace slip away when confronted with worldly pressure and we revert back to human reasoning of a situation.

Having been struggling with my own worldly pressures even after great moments of grace - I was challenged when the following words were spoken. They were spoken in reference to Our Lords journey, but they also spoke volumes to me. The speaker said, "Jesus was betrayed and then entered into His passion". They resonated with me because I too had been betrayed. For over twenty or more years, the pattern had been set for me to enter into my own passion. I guess some may call it the dark night of the soul. I am no theologian, but I know there is such a place.

Today my heart is finished breaking, no longer must I look backward or even forward - for there is no future that is visible to be seen in either - like an engine stalled on a railway line is how I would describe my feelings at this moment - stationary, rusting away in the conditions that surround me, the cold, the wind and the driving rain of life's cruel hand continuing to batter me.

Maybe it is time to just settle down and accept what is, for no longer can the dreams that were my hope, my future, any longer to be seen - many who were much stronger than I - took control of my life's dreams.

The sad thing was that when they had run their race with my dreams and where finished with them, they politely remarked that certain things only had a life span of five years anyway.

I believe they could never know, that what I had hoped for was not a dream for financial gain or recognition, but my over whelming inner joy was to share the very peace and knowledge that I had experienced in the knowing that Jesus my Savior was real.

A long time ago, I had asked Jesus to show me His Father, it happened at a prayer meeting while I was sitting with others gathered around a heater for the room was big and the night cold. In a quiet moment I lifted my head to gaze upon a picture hanging on a wall over the fireplace. Gazing at the picture of the Sacred Heart of Jesus, I asked him to please show me His Father. It was after this request, I became a little alarmed for having asked the question, as I remembered somewhere in scripture that Jesus had been asked this somewhere before, and His answer was something like this, *'If you have seen me, then you have seen the Father, for the Father is in me, and I am in the Father'.*

Sometime later after another meeting in the same place, I asked for prayer as I was leaving. Two ladies there offered to pray for me and one while praying placed her hands around my head (not on top of my head), and continued on speaking in English said, '*He is going to give you a great gift, something to do with the senses*'. These words gave me great joy because I somehow felt that everything was alright about the request I had made regarding showing me the Father."

I believe it was some time later that God in his mercy allowed me to receive the gift that had been spoken about. It was received after returning home from another smaller prayer group, when we were asked to make a note of the meeting. I remember it all so clearly going home finding pen and paper and sitting down to try my hand at making some notes regarding the meeting. All of a sudden I could hear these words flooding into my mind, each one no faster than I could write them. I continued to write the words as I was hearing them and as they finished, I just put away the pen and placed the written words into my bible thinking that that had been so easy.

I have shared with others what happened many times - but to continue to clarify it, I will add it here. On arriving at the home of one of the two ladies I was meeting with, we were asked if any of us had made some notes from last week's meeting, both the other ladies said that they had not made any.

It was then I remembered I had made some notes but was unsure if they were still in my Bible. I was encouraged to produce them and as I began to read what I had written, quietness descended upon the three of us - it was as if I was hearing these words for the first time. These words were so loving, so caring, so unlike anything I would have been able to write myself – or would have even had the courage to write for they were speaking in the first person, and Jesus our Lord was the speaker.

As we parted that night I was encouraged to again write down something in regards to our meeting hoping to keep some sort of a record to see what God had in line for the group next.

On arriving home I again took the pen and paper and sat down to make my notes. Just as before, without having to think - the words again appeared in my mind. All I had to do was to write them down. At the following weeks meeting the same peace descended engulfing us all as we listened to the words of the second night being read.

This happened at three consecutive meetings and after each meeting I began to become aware that maybe this was a special gift from God. The gift that had been prophesied some time earlier when a lady had placed her hands around my head and said, *'You will receive a great gift in this area something to do with the senses, He (the Lord) is saying it is a gift from His heart to your heart she said as she pointed to the picture of the Sacred Heart hanging over the fireplace'.*

After the three weeks of receiving the words following the prayer meetings, I was beginning to think that it would only happen when I returned from a prayer meeting. Then one day I got the courage to sit and ask the Lord if He would like me to listen and write. To my delight the words were immediately there and I would write everything I had heard and when they stopped, I would just close up the book and put down the pen.

The same thing began to happen at the prayer meetings, when I would hear the words and just speak them out so others there could hear them. I also found that on no part of mine, I could pray for people - even people I had never met before and there would always be words for them – always given with such love and understanding of the person being prayed for. I knew and I believe the people that I had prayed for understood it was not me that had the knowledge of their lives, their inner hurts or their levels of anxiety and stress. The words could only have come from the one who had created them and had great knowledge of everything in their lives and what they were going through.

I would see how they would be consoled as they realized that God knew them personally. People would often come back to me and ask again what had been said during the time of prayer when the Lord was giving them the words. But God in His great mercy would never leave me with this knowledge and I could always say honestly that I may remember a few words, but certainly not all, and most certainly not enough to make a guess of my own. I was always conscious that I must never change any word that I heard, or was given to say.

As time passed and many things happened, of which I was unaware of, my peace and joy began to fade, as I realized that many things were happening around me and many other things had been taken out of my control.

It is best to say things, were changing, others took over and began to run with ideas that they had felt had been laid upon their hearts to do. No longer did I have a place to fit into, either in the prayer group or even in the community. As I left that city, I remember speaking to the parish priest at the door of the church after mass and his remark has always remained with me for he said, "Maybe it is me that should be leaving, not you". I have often wondered about his remark as time has gone by for he was the chaplain to the Police Force in that area. As time passed, I began to realise that a lady from the Police Academy had been kind enough to type some of what I had written privately which had been given to a friend, who also was the instigator putting together the first of the writings into book form.

I believe in their goodness they had it put together by a group from a sheltered work shop run by the St Vincent de Paul. So strange how God allows his ways to work and how he can take people, place and situations to bring about change and encouragement, so people can see that he is really who he says he is.

When I started to receive the words, I was told that no one need know it was I that was taking them down so God told me to use the name, 'The Obedient One' and so I did this.

Sometime later, God told me it was alright now to use my real name in the writings. At this point when I told the priest what had been said things somehow changed. Things began to spiral out of control for me and for the next twenty or more years, the roller coaster has continued on. One day I would think I was on the top of the ride with everything in view for me to see and make sense of – then the ride would start up again, run at full pace downhill in the opposite direction. This caused everything that I thought was settled and in place, to end up like an upset jigsaw puzzle. And I was back searching for insight to all that had happened, with no answer for the past or even less understanding as to what was happening now. When I stepped off the ride at the gateway, there would be even more confusion than when I started the ride.

I would seek answers from those I thought would have the answers, but I was always met with a cold no-comment in reply. As time passed with no answers, I became aware that many people were open and ready to listen to what I would say, either by the words I was receiving to write, or the dreams I was shown. But alas, there would be no help given to me in return. I would witness many of the words

I had received slightly turned around to show that they were not exactly the same as mine or others added to them that changed the meaning of what I had written which allowed them to be given the meaning that others believed would suit them better.

No one would understand the great trial this was to cause me; it appeared I became a person who did not exist, while others continued to benefit from the gift I had been given or the name I possessed. When you are placed in this position you can only rely on God, for there is not another to give you comfort for what you know in your heart was the truth. For reasons of their own they all had to remain silent and anonymous.

Only last week at Mass I heard some words that gave me some comfort when it was mentioned that Jesus my Lord and savior, when he was betrayed – he then entered into his passion. I took comfort from the word betrayed, for I knew without a doubt I also had been betrayed by others. I do not name names or seek revenge, for they, I believe became pawns in the game that Satan was able to enter into. Telling all, as we are told in scripture, that he can turn himself into an angel of light and appear before men and women to make certain things appear good when in the end they only bring about death. Just as he outmaneuvered Adam and Eve in the garden with his ability to deceive them in telling them that by eating the apple they would have great knowledge and be like God himself.

Looking back, I see Satan's cunning hand in causing people to believe that it was Gods time to make us all one. Even Jesus could not do this, for he asked that the Father would keep safe all those he had been given, except the one that scripture had foretold would be lost (Judas the betrayer). Jesus said, *'Father I have kept safe all those you have given me, that none should be lost, I pray Father that you will make us one - just as I am in my Father, so that they may be in us* (Jn 17: 11-12). Maybe my words here are not exact, but it is how I remember it today.

When I wrote the words in the first little book I remember they said, 'You are all my children.' I guess many others believed that it might be the time of change when all will be one. Yet, as I wrote them I had no hesitation of their meaning that was, 'God who had created the universe and everything in it, had also created human life.' I am no psychic, historian or theologian but I immediately thought although human form had been developing long before Adam and Eve, it was not until they (Adam and Eve) were formed in God's image and likeness that the first persons appeared with body, mind, soul and spirit, so in these things God created them in His image and likeness.

I do not say we then look like God - but humans were given the gift of life only when God breathed the breath of life into his nostrils and the man began to live. (Genesis 2: 7-9) God planted a garden in Eden, in the East, and there he put the man he had formed. He made all kinds of beautiful trees grow there and produce good fruit. In the middle of the garden stood the tree that gives life and the tree that gives knowledge of what is good and what is bad."

(Gen: 3: 1-5) Human Disobedience:

The snake asked the women, "Did God really tell you not to eat fruit from any tree in the garden?"

"We may eat the fruit of any tree in the garden," the woman answered, "except the tree in the middle of it. God told us not to eat the fruit of that tree or even touch it; if we do, we will die."

The snake replied, "That's not true; you will not die."God said that because he knows that when you eat it, you will be like God and know what is good and what is bad."

(Gen: 3: 7)As soon as they had eaten it, they were given understanding and realized that they were naked; so they sewed fig leaves together and covered themselves. The disobedience to God's word caused Adam and Eve to lose their innocence.

We, I believe are given free will to accept the messages passed down through the centuries to remain faithful to God and His word- or – somehow we could get lost, become proud and headstrong, and believe that by eating of the apple we would as Eve thought, become wise and be like God.

I am reminded of this today, for I watched a conversation last evening on the television where a group of people were speaking about same sex marriages. There was a young well dressed, well presented, and well spoken man there, giving his opinion on the subject. He was so sure of his own opinion that his speech was so overpowering the others who tried to enter the conversation and have their voices heard. The young man continued to express his views and woe to anyone that did not agree with them. These people in his opinion were uneducated and needed to have someone explain it to them that things and people had *changed*.

That word again 'change' it seems to be popping up all over the place. Anyway the clincher for me was at the end of his speech, he wished the people were as educated as he in this matter, as he was a gay man and understood - and – who knew what needed doing in this area of change. He also ended on the note that he hoped many would recognize his political party and join them.

In amazement I thought all you need to tell us now is that Satan has handed you a *golden apple* and you decided to eat from it. (What happens next?) For we know what happened to Adam and Eve.

I am wondering why, with all this knowledge that has been eaten from the tree of knowledge – how much was consumed from the forbidden fruit and how much from the tree of knowledge that leads to wisdom. With courage and right judgment to fulfill Gods will from this wisdom that brings about, healing and peace.

I'm afraid all I can see is greed, anger, hatred, stress, division, separation and loneliness, with people not being able to believe or trust another. Somehow I cannot see where changes can take credit for bringing about healing and peace. Even the weather, all over the world is spiraling into chaos to cause such damage to homes lives animals and crops without even a shot being fired people are displaced from their comfort zones.

Lord, on this evenings news I could see great support from both political parties for the same sex marriage bill. It was as I watched that I felt a great heaviness come over me and for a time I felt helpless as I believed the yes vote will get it.

It was not so much that the yes vote would win – rather it was a feeling that we and this land Australia will be given our own wakeup call after it happens. And I felt that the disaster or whatever was or is to come, will be out of our control.

I pray for mercy Lord, but whatever is your will – I give you glory honor and praise for it. My Lord, if my thinking is on the wrong path please return me to the right path. Yet, as I watched our Prime Minister and the opposition leader both proudly supporting this bill it was then that the pride that they were portraying was what scared me the most. For the people who have decided this type of lifestyle is for them are (in my opinion - and I hope I am wrong God), appear to be very well versed and have a very loud voice.

What will happen next? – Only you know!

Please protect those that love you and keep them safe from Satan's lies.

I make this prayer in Jesus Name. Amen

Words Received

Go in peace Pam, you have foreseen the future this night but be not afraid, for the enemy of the Lord is not in control as many may think. He has been allowed to menace for some time but the battle he has been waging will come to naught.

My Prayer

My Lord and My God, open my eyes that I may walk more closely with you this day. Whatever time you grant me to live on this earth, please let me use it to come closer to you. I want my life to become a place where the angels and saints of heaven become my true friends so that when we finally meet the joy will be great.

There has been many times in my life when I have withdrawn into my shell or cave, all because I somehow wanted another to tell me that my way of thinking and acting was okay with you. Today Lord, all I want is to know you personally and to follow you so closely that in your great mercy you will inspire me to be more obedient to you and your word. If, my Lord I can do this, I pray it will bring others to you also.

Many have given over their entire lives to you to show their love and desire to walk with you and to follow your teachings. How I desire to be one of them. Only by your grace can anyone really know you.

Hold my hand please Lord Jesus – for I am becoming older and frailer – but that is in body only, for my heart, soul, mind and spirit is young in wanting to come closer to you to really know you, My Lord and My God.

Lord Jesus a long time ago after visiting a certain church, I was given in one of my times of writing the following words. Strange, they came from Saint Peter the one to whom you gave the keys of your Holy Roman Catholic Church to.

The words I believe I heard were as spoken by Saint Peter; *'I don't think she can do it – but we will give her a go.'*

How I pray that when I reach heaven and see your holy disciple Saint Peter he will tell me that whatever he thought I could not do – that in fact with your help I have been able to stand before the powers of hell, only because you were at my side and by your great mercy I survived.

My Lord, I come to you humbly seeking guidance and direction from you this day. Allow my eyes and ears to be open with spiritual insight to see the enemy before he can do any more damage to me or my loved ones. Allow me to come home into your holy house and find true peace within her.

My love for your Holy Roman Catholic Church just grows more each day – especially as I watch it being persecuted – and being humiliated by the sins of all – who follow you – but I wonder if they will not remember the words you showed me yesterday morning.

"Let whoever is without sin, cast the first stone" (Jn 8: 7) – great words to reflect on during this period of time in the world today – for we are all sinners.

6.
DREAMS

My Prayer

Good morning Lord. During the night, I lay awake thinking of all the things that have happened over the years before and after receiving the Holy Spirit in my life and the one thing that stood out was the dream I was given all those years ago in Goulburn. As I recall I had just come out of the church and was walking just a short distance down the footpath, when my legs became weak and I sank to the ground, my husband and son were with me, and I called out to them asking if they knew what was happening.

In the vision, I had seen appear on a wall a big dark wooden cross but there was nothing on the cross. I then was shown another cross and on this cross was a symbol of our Lady holding the baby Jesus in her arms, just like in the icon of Our Lady of Perpetual Succour.

As I looked, I could see people throwing things towards this cross, towards the Mother and her Child as if they wanted to dislodge them both from the cross. By this time they had almost removed both of them and they were just hanging slightly over the edge. I cried out, 'What are they doing to the Blessed Mother?' Recalling this point, I fell to the ground quite distressed and woke from the vision.

Again, in the same place, I had a second dream, but this time I was on the opposite side of the church. I was standing with some people and we appeared to be like a "MASH unit." I could hear a bell tolling in the next village and it seemed to be a warning that the village had fallen to invaders and we would be the next to come under their attack. Looking out at the scene in front of me, I could see an elderly knight in armour on his horse leaving the battle and moving away. The strange thing was he was sitting backward on his horse, as if looking back towards the village where the bells had rang. As he passed by he looked towards me, not speaking, but his eyes seemed to say, 'You are the last ones left to defend this place' and here I woke from the dream.

Another time I remember being in that church, I came across the two statues that had been taken down from the top of the church for restoration. They appeared so big, as they now stood on the floor inside the church door. I was drawn to them immediately and seeing Saint Paul standing there with sword in hand, I immediately went to him because of the sword representing the word of God and his writings.

But for some reason, I was pulled away back to the statue of Saint Peter. Now gazing close up at this statue for the first time, I noticed that there at Saint Peters feet stood a Rooster; I guess it is good to be reminded how that one rooster can stir up a lot of regrets in our lives. If Only?

Laying awake last night, I believe I had to start to write again all that I heard and possibly God will show me what if anything He wants done with it. 'So this is my yes to you Father God. Amen'.

7.
ALL SAINTS DAY

My Prayer

Today is the anniversary of my mother's funeral Father God, and I would like to thank you for allowing me to attend Mass this morning. I thank you for the Mass -my Mother, and for Jesus my Lord. Amen.

Words Received

Dine in my kingdom Pam whenever you can. You will be well rewarded for your faithfulness. Others are coming to understand all that I have been allowing you to see for so long. The enemy has taken over in the world with much gusto - puffing and ranting and spewing out poison with fire into the hearts of so many people. These people are being fueled by his poison and now he is gathering an army of servants for himself. He has told them that this is the way to go, to take control of all that surrounds them regardless of the cost to the innocent ones who may accidently be caught in the way.

I am the beloved of my Father - and all that I tell you has come from Him. Do not be afraid to remain faithful to what you know in your heart to be true. You must understand that you have been put in this position so other's will see your faithfulness and remember, that their own faith needs to return to the point that they see in yours.

The angel will gather around you, those you will be truly able to trust. I will never leave you and there will be many more wonderful things for you to enjoy in my name.

Delight in the fact that I am opening the eyes of others to see you as you are - the way I see you. I believe today you will be allowed to come follow me in all my glory. Go in peace Pam.

I love you Lord and thank you for everything. Amen.

Melbourne Cup

Two days ago the Melbourne cup was run - on reflecting on things that have always stood out for me about this day, was the stormy weather that somehow engulfed that day. The other being the champagne, wine, and beer that flows at the racecourse, as well as the awful behavior of some that attend where it appears all loss of modesty for dress and behavior disappears from many - young and old - who seem to lose all sense of decorum for themselves and anyone around them. Not only do we appear to be dumbing down in dress, but also dumbing down in composure and actions, not to mention speech. These are just my own observations, so I know many would howl me down for thinking this way – and would say they are just having fun.

As the race unfolded I became aware of the irony of it, as the winning jockey and horse was lead back into the winning circle. My mind flew back to the running of the 2009 Melbourne Cup when the jockey that day experienced his first cup win and the last day I recall betting on the race, and I had done so simply because of the name of the horse. It was called Shocking and I have a niece who would always say. 'No one could say the word shocking like her Nan, my mother.

Here we are eight years on and this very same jockey appeared in the winning circle riding the winning horse whose name was Rekindling. It was rather odd as I listened to his interview with the media, they seemed to indicate that his career had not been going well since his first win.

Hearing these comments, I thought about all that had taken place in my life and in the lives of my loved ones and extended family members since then, and thought Mum's "shocking" would cut us all to the bone were she still with us today.

Putting away the past and come to 2017 Melbourne Cup and look at the same scene (horse and jockey) and the name of the winning horse Rekindling – I pray that it is the sign of all of Mum's and my extended family to rekindle friendships without anger or bitterness and to start again in peace and love with honesty and truth for all.

Words Received

Don't dally Pam, pick up the pen and write what I tell you. Now, go forth in my name and proclaim the truth. Others have tried and caused such a mess. Greed became too powerful and they were succumbed by its charm. I tell you solemnly that they are all in a state of confusion, not knowing what will be revealed and how it will affect them.

I tell you solemnly, that regardless of what they will try and do to fix things it will not be successful, for my hand has ran out of patience and it will no longer be held back. Be brave for I tell you they are more frightened of you than you need be of them.

Holy is my hand and I will protect my own in whatever way I want to. Go into my holy word and read there all that is about to be revealed. You will find my words in Jeremiah 27 - Jeremiah has been listening to your prayers and he also is counting on you to return my people to me. Go in peace and listen more often.

I was encouraged to read Paul's second letter to Timothy.

Timothy 3: 10-17, 4: 1-5. Last Instructions:

"But you have followed my teaching, my conduct, and my purpose in life; you have observed my faith, my patience, my love, my endurance, my persecutions, and my sufferings. You know all that happened to me in Antioch, Iconium, and Lystra, the terrible persecutions I endured! But the Lord rescued me from them all.

Everyone who wants to live a godly life in union with Christ Jesus will be persecuted; and evil persons and impostors will keep on going from bad to worse, deceiving others and being deceived themselves. But as for you, continue in the truths that you were taught and firmly believe. You know who your teachers were, and you remember that ever since you were a child, you have known the Holy Scriptures, which are able to give you the wisdom that leads to salvation through faith in Christ Jesus. All Scripture is inspired by God and is useful for teaching the truth, rebuking error, correcting faults, and giving instruction for right living, so that the person who serves God may be fully qualified and equipped to do every kind of good deed".

4:1-5

"In the presence of God and of Christ Jesus, who will judge the living and the dead, and because he is coming to rule as King, I solemnly urge you to preach the message, to insist upon proclaiming it (whether the time is right or not), to convince, reproach, and encourage, as you teach with all patience. The time will come when people will not listen to sound doctrine, but will follow their own desires and will collect for themselves more and more teachers who will tell them what they are itching to hear. They will turn away from listening to the truth and give their attention to legends. But you must keep control of yourself in all circumstances; endure suffering, do the work of a preacher of the Good News, and perform your whole duty as a servant of God".

Words Received

Hurry child, hurry - go now and do as I ask.

Heal My People Pam - They have come to the edge of the cliff. They must either turn around to face again the demons they have been running from, or they will continue on and will fall over the cliff into the abyss that stands before them.

Holy they must become Pam, Holy all people who have pulled the wool over their own eyes in order not to see that many of their actions they believed they were doing good, and serving me, were no more than selfish desires conjured up by their own imagination.

Daughter, hurry and write this upon your computer so they will see that there is still time to repent and turn around their lives.

Hurry Child, Hurry, go now and do as I say.

My Prayer

I, Pam am a daughter of the Lord God Most High and I follow my Lord and Saviour Jesus Christ – Under the banner of the Holy Roman Catholic Church of which I have been a member of (by God's grace) from the cradle and I pray will be until the grave.

Put the Warning Up

No wonder God told me to hurry and put this warning up. I am the one the Lord God most high had told me to call myself the Obedient One. I did this as asked - but there came a time later on when I was told I could now put my own name forward, but when I approached the people who knew all about what had been happening, I was immediately shunned and no more was said.

Today I found this website called - Roman Catholic Women Priests.

My goodness, how much more offensive for me to see this, when it is the one thing as a Roman Catholic Woman, that through my writings, I was told how Satan was taking great delight in seeing almighty God being offered the most holy sacrifice of the Mass in remembrance of his beloved son being crucified on a cross for the forgiveness of sin, being offered to him by his second creation - women servants.

Where are the real men who should be standing up against Satan and his cohorts? Why are you not defending the great and wonderful sacraments given to the church to guide and help with salvation for the people of God?

Have you men become so scared of the women's liberation that you are no longer able to speak - why are you as men, not living up to the gender you were born to represent – not just in serving God in his holy house, but men of God who should be caring and protecting women and children who are the weaker gender.

We are not weaker in Gods eyes just because we are women – rather we have a very important role to play as women and if women read the bible they would understand what it said and be at peace with their femininity; to be loved by God and rewarded by him in the roles we play as women, and that does not mean that we have to try to be men.

I have been hidden away by God for this day and my courage has now just been developed. And like my saviour Jesus Christ when his anger of righteousness and love for his father and his father's house, became just too much for him to witness, he made a whip and overturned the money lenders tables and drove them and their animals out of the temple saying,

"Stop turning my Father's house into a market place" Jn 2: 16.

And now, I have no qualms anymore about what I am saying for I have been silenced for too long and now it is my turn to say what I think.

The enemies of my Father's house are about to be exposed, for they would not listen to the warnings that had been sent to them for so long. They just believed that day would not come for them, for they were far too worldly to have to take any notice – and they believed they were well guarded by their cohorts.

All I can now say is, everything is in God's hands and I pray he will have mercy on us all. Amen.

8.
MY HELPERS

My Prayer

Come Holy Spirit and renew in me the gift of love.

My ways, are not your ways Lord, but today, I want your ways to become my ways. I surrender my ways this very moment as I sit writing this prayer before the very throne of the Risen Lord. I come before that throne this moment in my mind's eye and kneeling before the King of Kings, the Risen Lord Jesus Christ, as He sits at his Father's right hand and humbly prostrate myself before His majesty, seeking his will for my life this day and all the days for the rest of my life.

I remember also today, that it seems a life time ago that I was told that I would be given three helpers on my journey of life, they being, Saint Joan of Arc, Saint John of the Cross, and Raphael the Archangel. As I ponder these saints today, I remember the great feats they did to remain faithful to the one I kneel before in my mind's eye.

Saint Joan, although a young woman, I believe was given the grace and courage to ride with an army of men into battle. To hold high the standard of her Holy Roman Catholic faith believing in her heart that what she had been told to do by the heavenly beings, was what she must do.

I can understand how that feeling pushes you on and gives you more courage than anyone, including yourself, could imagine.

You watch those around you walk away and leave, even those who you believed were true friends. Then you become ignored by the very Church that you love, everything including your own family no longer able to understand you and the inner stress that has engulfed you. No longer living in an area where you could go freely into a church to sit quietly before the Lord in the presence of the tabernacle –but rather, a hall only opened on the weekend in which to give praise to the Almighty God.

I felt like a ship on the ocean being tossed about by the waves. It appeared that everything that I had taken for granted and loved in my closeness and love of God and His Holy Church had been taken away from me. I entered into a new garden that was being planted, in which I soon found that there was no place for me or my way of thinking.

I watched as each door closed against me and each of my previous thoughts were now being distributed by others. I had been encouraged by one to go and join a prayer group.

But I can only pray that when that advice was given, they too were in the midst of the cloud that Satan has shrouded everyone in. I pray that they did not know how hurtful that comment had been, for I had even started a prayer group in my own home and for a long time many came – but over time, it seemed they came and took what they wanted and then went on their journey to begin whatever they were doing.

I even started a prayer group in our own parish church, but came to realise that even that had become infiltrated and their mission to shut it down became successful.

There was so much secrecy, no one seemed to be able to tell the truth – silence was the vow each had taken and no-one was about to open their mouths. But whenever I did attend a meeting, it would not be long before what I had said, was appearing in places that I knew I had no connection with. I began to think that I was being recorded in what I said and did at these meetings. And, I felt others were taking them to use as their own. I would not have minded that if they had only used the words Lord that I believed you had given me - but they did not understand them and took them and interpreted them the way they believed they should be. This Lord is why I could no longer attend other prayer meetings.

I believe with all my being, that the words I was given were from you Lord, and I remembered what Holy Scripture had said, "Don't throw your pearls before swine for they will only trample them underfoot" (Mt 7: 6). I believe the words I was given, either to write or speak, were your pearls and I was not guarding them as I should.

I felt I was the meat in a sandwich, on one side I would hear the Lord and wanted so much to do His will, while on the other – I was so closely guarded, locked in and hidden away with so little communication from the outside world. If only while I was in that place, I had been able to take the opportunity to grow closer to you Father, Son and Holy Spirit, and just wait with patience to be released from my prison maybe, it could have been a little more bearable.

I believe today Satan tried so hard to bring about my down fall, because in the end, even my close friends began to believe that all that had happened, and was continuing to happen to bring down the Holy Roman Catholic Church, had been my fault. Satan's biggest lie and his downfall was to tell others to tell me that all I needed to do to regain all that I had lost, was to change my name or my religion.

I believe in my heart that was the day that Satan over stepped the line in his pride and exposed what he had been working on to bring about such disaster for myself and my family. That was the day I believe that the cloud began to split open and the new ray of sunlight from God's mercy began to appear in the words and voices of those around me whom I loved. I praise you God, for your mercy and protection for myself and my loved ones.

Saint Joan, you were a defender of The Holy Roman Catholic Church and its faith, within your native country of France – but just like Jesus your Saviour you were wrongly judged. You were burnt at the stake by your peers, because they had no eyes to see the works of Satan and the path he was preparing to bring about much disaster. So many people become blind when Satan pulls across the cloud of lies to stop them from seeing with both their eyes and their mind.

Saint Joan was a mighty warrior and fighter and God I believe gave her to me, to be my protector and a model for my life. However, it soon became apparent to me, that others had quickly seized upon her image for their own financial interest.

Saint Joan was taken from my grasp as a helper and guide and became the standard bearer for those seeking their own interests in promoting war history filling libraries with tales of courage while others fabricated images of her horse and fighting apparel to improve their bank balances.

In this day and age, we have many scientists and medical professionals trying to un-cloud the minds of the people of the earth, but each day many more, young and old, are losing their ability to think clearly, the fog that the cloud produces, is now becoming big business. People are being told each day about how to keep their minds healthy and at peace. But for those whom Satan sends a spirit of lies and fear towards each day; their lives are lives of misery – no longer do people have to be locked away in dungeons to be deprived of the light. All Satan has to tell them is that there is no light outside of what he is telling them, so he herds them like sheep into mobs and tells them that to stay safe, they must stay close together and not speak to anyone in case they are exposed to the light and grace of God.

Satan can change himself into an angel of light, the message he comes with appears to many to be true and he does not need a drum to beat, or a trumpet to blow, a football to kick, a bat to hit a ball with, a gun or a knife or fancy fast cars, horses, food, drink, or holidays to entice people to come follow him. He has a whole world of marketers out there to do it for him, each one only too happy to outdo the other with their offerings 2 Cor 11: 14.

I do feel for all those people who try to market in all honesty and keep their own integrity and may God bless and protect them always in the name of our saviour the Lord Jesus Christ, I make this prayer. Amen.

Oh dear, what a troubled world we live in when first people practice to deceive, for we know no good will come from it, for Satan the father of lies is the one behind it. I don't like to write this, but those who practice to deceive and lie are showing who they are following and listening to, it is, Satan, the Father of all lies.

I was once shown in a vision an angel stepping out from a cave and stepping into a cloud. At the time of the vision, I was unable to understand its meaning, but today I believe I do, for Satan has taken over the airwaves. There is so much now that happens to cause people to be separated and herded into small groups of their own way of thinking. Some have found themselves imprisoned where they would never have gone, if the airwaves had not been open to expose such awful sights and acts, that would only have been acted out in the cover of darkness are now daily being acted out on our televisions, computers and iPads - daily just a flick of the switch and the instrument lights up to produce such actions.

I believe the greatest lie Satan has been able to sell to the world today is pornography and violence. The porn in many cases is carried out through the airwaves that enter into a person's home and life, maybe unbeknown to others sharing the house which will over time come to see the reaction of the one Satan is feeding with these images to pull down their defences and numb their conscience and soon they began to no longer feel guilty or embarrassed about what they are doing.

Even if this is so, and they walk away from knowing what is right in the sight of God, I pray they will stop and understand that God will never take away their free will to do such things, but if they are opening and making entry into that house or family for the spirit of lust to gain access, then it is almost too sad to think about.

In Holy Scripture we are told, "If anyone should cause a small child to lose their soul, it would be better for that person to take a large mill stone and tie it around their neck and cast themselves into the water"(Mt 18: 6). Pretty hard words to hear but so often of late, the only words we hear preached are love. We know God is love but He is also a God of justice, and He will hear and defend the cry of the poor, the innocent, and the people who truly follow him. Those who do not just talk the talk, but those who both talk the talk and walk the walk in speaking the truth in God's name, will set the captives free from the lies and deception of Satan and his cohorts who have taken captive the airwaves.

My Prayer

My Lord and my God – I have come to seek mercy and to ask for forgiveness for not having written in this book earlier.

Only if you want me to do so now Lord – I humbly seek to do your will and seek your guidance.

In the name of Jesus, I thank you. Amen.

Words Received

My hand has already been raised and they are in disarray Pam. They did not think I would do this to them, they all believed they were in the right. But you know I have been warning them for a long time now and they have not listened. Rather they have been gathering together to try and start a new project in which they planned to do more damage than the last one.

Come, you will be set free from their world of lies and deception. Gather your strength for the last battle and you will see them retreat forever.

They are unsure of what you intend to do, so be wise – say nothing and I will expose them for you without you having to say anything.

Go in peace.

Thank You Jesus, Amen.

My Prayer

Come Holy Spirit of the living God, please fall afresh on my family, and please fall afresh on me. Please give me your orders – I promise to do what you ask of me, and promise to accept all that you allow to happen to me - only please let me know your Holy Will. In Jesus name, I seek your mercy and forgiveness. Amen.

Words Received

The Holy Hill of the Lords presence has been invaded by infidels Pam. They are in the process of destroying my holy house. Many entered in under the cover of darkness, while others entered in broad daylight. They were the ones that Satan had changed into an angel of light. Showing great insight into the troubled times, but all the while behind the scene they were stirring the water to make trouble for all to see. They have had their time of being in the spotlight without their true colors being revealed.

Show mercy to that one who has caused you so much trouble, for things will change for them and for others who have been confused by the light that was shining so brightly upon your family for the very reason to confuse and divide you all. Never again, will the enemy be able to deceive you or your loved ones. Go in peace to start your day for I am with you. Amen.

My Prayer

Please allow me to receive your wisdom and guidance this day Lord God most high. There are many questions still unanswered in my mind, and still even more paths before me. Please, don't let me go down the wrong one this day and just waste time in having to come back. In the holy name of your beloved son I ask for this wisdom. Amen

Words Received

When the dust settles today, the enemy will be exposed. Show patience for a little longer - so much is happening behind the scenes and you must allow it to happen in order to expose all.

You will be guided by my hand as you open your computer and those who understand why you continue to search, will come to your aid, for they see how determined you have been in listening to my word and following my instructions. Hold on to all that you know is truth and this truth will set you free. Go in my peace, to love, and serve, your God. Amen

9
JUSTICE

My Prayer

New Zealand

Yesterday evening as I turned on the television, I was confronted by the terrible attack in New Zealand. I believe forty nine people lost their lives when a man opened fired on them while they were praying in a mosque in New Zealand. This attack has shaken the world, as New Zealand is a very peaceful country. The man charged for carrying out the attack was an Australian.

For all those people who lost their lives, I ask that they may rest in peace and a perpetual light shine upon them. In Jesus holy name I make this prayer. Amen.

My Lord and my God, I don't know what to say. Please, have mercy on all who cause division and hatred in your name. Please send your Holy Spirit afresh to hearts that have grown cold and no longer bow down to worship you. Don't allow the enemy to deceive your people – those who are called by your name. Amen. What can I do – if anything - to change my own heart and bring it into line with your Sacred Heart and the way you think?

Words Received

The willing heart that seeks my justice will receive it. Those who have been causing the injustice in the world by seeking to be important in the eyes of the world will be the very ones to bring about shame for themselves and much regret for them and many who listened to them. The anger that they are feeling at this moment will be nothing to the fear that will grip them when they realise they will be exposed. Go in peace.

My Prayer

My Lord and my God, regardless of all that has been said in the past - tonight I ask if you still want to speak with me - just as I am at this moment?

Words Received

Pam, they have again covered our words (the words I gave you) and they believed you would not notice. Daughter, I am becoming quite concerned about certain people that may get in your way. I will allow you to put down this message this night and if anyone tries to interfere with it, you will be shown and you will need to come forward and ask the question, as to why this is being done, do not let them interfere with what I am asking of you. I tell you solemnly that what I give to you is to be used by you and not by those who in the past have infiltrated the written words and claimed them as their own.

Lord, this is quite concerning and I am unsure of what I should do; please come to my aid.

The Devil has been roaming around now for quite some time he has been trying to turn himself into an angel of light but this time his antics will not be tolerated. Just like the Pharisees of old they gather together to try and bring down the good person, knowing that the good person will try and give them sympathy as to their motives. I tell you solemnly my daughter the tricks that were being used in the past will not work now. The light is being shown directly upon them and if they don't want to be caught in its headlights, they will have to run for cover and to do it quickly. You were full of sympathy for them and they had covered their identity and continued to persecute you and My Holy Roman Catholic Church.

Do not trust them my daughter, for they will blow like the wind in whatever way the enemy prods them. Tell them enough is enough, and they must leave right now.

My Prayer

A writing from the past but oh so important for me to remember today: I ask the world, please don't take or use my words even if you can access them.

My Lord and My God they have tried to silence me for far too long – please come to my aid and allow me to bring your Holy Name forward.

Anyone who is opposing me in this manner please give me eyes to see them and wisdom to know how to deal with them and any situation that may arise. Please hear my prayer, in Jesus Name I pray. I thank you Jesus for your great mercy Amen.

Words Received

Align your heart with mine Pam, for the day has come to bring down their house of cards and the tree house that has been built to house them. Angels and saints have been waiting for this day to arrive so that they may do the work I have prepared for them to do.

So many believe they are untouchable and hold all the trump cards but how silly they will look when I send the wind to blow down their hiding place – and hiding places they have been. My hand told you yesterday where they were hiding, so be unafraid when you see them scattered today.

If they do not Pam, there will be no more time for they have been the cause of many people suffering greatly.

My Prayer

The Greed of the People

Oh Father God, I cannot seem to be able to understand why so many people voted for the political party they put into govern our country last weekend. We know that this party stands for power and wealth. Yet this morning we have a man from the Salvation Army expressing his concerns on the television regarding the poverty of so many older people – especially women over sixty who have been divorced or widowed and who have not been able to save enough for their retirement, because they gave their time in looking after family and were out of the work force and unable to secure enough superannuation to live on towards the end of their working life.

I have tried to think about this outcome and to my surprise my mind became open to what I have been witnessing since last weekend.

I watched seat after seat falling to the Liberal/National Coalition Party.

So that being said, the people voted for this government – one person in three voted for the Labor party in NSW, and one person in four voted for Labor in Queensland. So that would have to be a very convincing victory to the Liberal/National Coalition Party.

My concern in listening to the Prime Minister's campaign speeches is that I only really heard him speak about two policies, one being jobs and growth, the other to bring the economy into surplus. These were the only two things he was offering to the people. Yet not once, did I hear him say how he was going to achieve their outcome. I imagine he will invest in building some infrastructure to create jobs for people to get income from. That would be good as long as we give those jobs to the people who are already seeking work. But will that make up for the number that do not pay any taxes and where the money never seems to make it into a cash register – but rather vanishes quietly and secretly into people's back pockets. Nice for those who do that and are not caught by the tax man – but the day of reckoning will come Lord – if not in this life but surely when they kneel before you to be judged. We believe this, for we are told in Holy Scripture, that every knee will bow before you in this manner (Phil 2: 10-11).

It was revealed by media reporting that when our Prime Minister was congratulated by the American President he said how like his own unexpected election our prime Minister's victory was.

One of the things they discussed was the war in Iran. How worrying is that, for everyone knows that Iran will not back down with bullying or threats. And Australia and other countries have had troops fighting in the Middle East for over twenty years now, with no real outcome for peace.

The party that was in opposition to the government in this election had gone with polices to try and help the poorer people living in this country. They offered dental assistance for those who could not afford it. They wanted the young children to be able to attend childcare earlier – which would allow their mothers more time to try and secure more super-annuation for their own retirement.

They could see that the wealthy were becoming greedier and were robbing their workers of wages that should have been paid – threatening them that unless they took a pay cut and worked for less, the business would go bust and there would be no jobs at all.

Threats, threats and more threats - from people who were lining up to purchase not their first home - but their fourth, fifth or even sixth, and expecting someone to pay for it with inflated rent to cover their loan.

All I can think is the amount of greed that has entered people's hearts and has expressed itself since the election is amazing. The Banks have regrouped, and their share prices have risen, and even though the people witnessed this during the enquiry into their conduct – there will never be anyone now held to answer for their actions or made answerable for their crimes – for the banks have been let off the hook.

I heard the opposition treasurer say this morning that he had budgeted for money to come from wealthy people to try and help the poor. But the people did not want that – so he said, they would have to look again at how the Labor Party looked at the elections. Especially about how they viewed what the people wanted.

Could that mean that Labor will give away the people with no-voice and follow the path of the Liberal/National

Coalition Party? Lord, I mentioned earlier that it is over twenty years ago now since the war in the Middle East began and I believe our Australian personnel have been involved there ever since.

It is also about the same time since you had us move from Goulburn to where we live now in Canberra.

This morning as I write this I realise just how things changed for my life on arriving here. But you know all about that – you heard me crying out for help, and for answers, and had you not been there, I just don't know what would have happened. The world around me seemed to be going mad. The pace of the runaway train became faster and faster, until all one could do was to hang on tightly and hope not to fall under its powerful wheels. I somehow feel this morning that it has somehow slowed down just long enough for people of all persuasions of politics to catch their breath – and maybe even those like me who have no voice, to be able to stop for a while and listen to the silence.

My concern is, for over those twenty years or more we have been glorifying war. Building bigger museums to house and display such outcomes. All people wanted it seemed to me, was to display their ancestors both here and overseas as heroes. Yet those who had returned from those terrible places of war did not even want to talk about it, even to their loved ones.

They just wanted to forget, and never go back there again. Yet we seem to show war as something of a hero status thing to do. Please don't get me wrong I feel all those who have had to endure war and return from it, are indeed heroes but heroes who would sooner not to have gone at all. I would say that those who send others to war should be made to accompany them into the warzone, and if they did - would they be as keen to send others.

Not only have we been glorifying such wars, but the entertainment industry has indulged itself in this business - from Lord of the Rings etc. to just gaming on the internet. I would have to ask the film and gaming makers, when they let this terrible spirit of hatred, fear, war, death and greed out into the airwaves, were they aware that this is the evil ones domain. And collide they will, the media and the newspapers etc., will make sure that they will report only what they want the people to hear.

One of yesterday's newspapers printed a picture of our newly elected Prime Minister claiming he was 'The Messiah from the Shire,' or words similar to that. He himself said he believed in miracles and I guess his success was really one of those miracles. You see the future, Lord Jesus Christ, I ask you to please protect those who truly love you and follow you, not just in words but by the way they live their lives. People who have heard your word and wish to follow you by wanting peace and justice for all people of good will.

I know you came to bring such good news to the earth, to set free from it the many voices that have cried out to you from where their blood has fallen into the soil from the hands of the unjust.

Many innocent people have died in war and for other reasons from the hands of evil people and they are calling on God to hear their story and be their defender even from the grave.

Oh Father God, I hope I am wrong but it would appear to me that the people have moved away from listening to what Jesus our Lord came to teach us, even after he suffered and died to give us the opportunity to know you his Father and your great mercy. It somehow seems we do not think about the reason why he came and what price he had to pay for making reparation for our sins in order that the gates of heaven could be opened again to souls.

I know you are a God of mercy Father God, but I also know that you are a God of justice and there will be a Day of Judgment and reckoning for all. When our whole life will be laid bare and we will see for ourselves what we have done with the life and time that we were given on this earth and how we used it – will we feel happy to knee before our saviour Jesus Christ, or will we be hanging our head in shame and with remorse. Each day as I grow closer to that judgment day, I wonder just how ready I am for that meeting. That is the question I ask myself today as I write these words, yet

I hope and pray for God's mercy upon my life and my actions within that life.

I wanted so much to speak about how real you are and how you have your hand on all things. But there came a time when the world sped up and there appeared to be no more time for listening quietly and reflecting upon you and all that you had done - including the mercy that you were showing us, by not destroying us for our sinfulness.

Today, I look back believing you are just as much with us, but that you have stepped back and left us to wander as children in this new wilderness. You allowed Moses and the tribes you led out of Egypt to wander for forty years in that wilderness, even though they were only (I am led to believe), eleven miles from where they were going.

Have you left us also to wander in this wilderness Father God? You said that all that had failed to honour you there in the desert with Moses would have to die before the next generation would be allowed to come out of that desert.

Father God, these are my thoughts, if they are wrong then please I ask for the guidance always from the Holy Spirit to teach me all things and to help me to remember all things. I invite you Holy Spirit the third person and God of the Trinity to open my mind to enable me to write what is proper, honest and true. Will I see the things I have been waiting to see Father God, or will my time run out before I see what I believe you told me would happen.

I make this prayer in Jesus Holy Name. Amen.

10.
HIS VOICE

My Prayer

If today you hear His voice, harden not your heart.

Good morning Lord God, thank you for bringing into being this new day. Thank you also for bringing me into this new day. I can only hope and pray that I will not waste this special day, but will be able to accomplish something that I can offer to you as thanksgiving for my life.

Yesterday I spoke to you about many things, especially about our country's elections. Today Lord I hope my thoughts will take me on a new path in which I can bring about more understanding for myself or anyone else who may one day wish to read them.

'My beloved is mine and my banner over her is love.'

Lord, these words from a song I remember from so long ago have just invaded my mind and what a lovely image of peace, security and feeling of protection they bring from my Heavenly Father.

Thank you Holy Spirit for helping me to remember, Amen.

Now, I must be more alert because of the new words that have just crossed my mind. They are, *'If today you hear His voice, harden not your heart.'*

When I hear the phrase His voice a few different ideas are conjured up in my mind. The first is an image of a little Jack Russel Terrier dog sitting next to a gramophone. Funnily enough this was an advertisement for a British Major record label, and it was called *His Master's Voice.*

The second idea is that, in today's world there are so many voices speaking, singing, calling loudly and offering opinions, that it is sometimes hard to hear yourself think over their racket. Listening to certain people within groups, I notice those who always want to be the loudest voice there, they do not even let another in the group finish their sentence before they are offering their opinion on how it should be fixed. Regardless of the above two, there is a voice that I would like to comment on more fully.

The Voice of the Holy Spirit of God that helps us to remember all things and who teaches us all things, it is that special voice that can cut through all other voices and thoughts and brings our own spirit to a standstill. It is so calm, loving and unmistakable. What a privilege it is to hear that voice of the Spirit of God, as it opens up your being to the wonder of God's word. Alleluia thank you Holy Spirit, and because you have told me to listen and not harden my heart, which I could easily have done after all that I had heard and read lately.

It is in obedience to that word I humbly ask for your directions and understanding, for how my heart should return to you and listen to what you are saying.

Strange as I am writing this, I see in my mind's eye a small country town that I have travelled through on many occasions. The name of the town is called Harden; it is in the Hilltop Shire in New South Wales, Australia. When I was quite a young girl, many years ago now, I remember hearing a visiting priest from America make a comment about this town. He said, "Today I travelled through a town called Harden. Why would anyone call a town Harden"?

Well Lord, today you have told me, if today I hear your voice then not to harden my heart. I will try and obey by saying, if by remembering the priests description of this town as Harden if by some chance it has left negative feelings in myself towards this place Lord, please allow my heart to set it free, so my own heart may be set free also to work and distribute my blood freely through my body according to the way you designed it to work. Without becoming hardened, as hearts are known to do as they work so hard all our life, pumping away causing the muscle to become hard.

Gee Lord, this is just some of the things that you brought to my mind as I sat down to write today.

Thank You.

My Prayer

My Lord, you once told me I was a slow learner and that I still had a lot to learn; that was quite a long time ago now. I remember it clearly, and oh, how true your words were. Even today, be it ever so slowly, I am still trying to seek your will for my life, even with the knowledge that I am getting older and I am afraid of running out of time to do something that will remain behind me to tell others how much I love you, and encourage them to believe that all that you have told us was real and true. Each day I watch as the world and the people become more foreign to my way of thinking and the way I would love for them to act. I guess I can only hope that one day I will be able to express my thoughts on paper at least in a satisfactory way that others will see that what I say is truly coming from the faith I have in you my Lord Jesus Christ the only beloved son of the Father. You are the one who all those years ago, heard my simple prayer when I asked you to show me your Father.

Lord Jesus, have I ever really thanked you for showing me your Father? Many people knew and know you in a very personal way, and loved you greatly and rightly so.

One of my sisters was one of those people and I remember her always telling us of the blessing you gave her on the day she finished attending Mass on the Nine First Fridays of the month. I remember clearly how she called with great excitement from the back yard of our home saying, "Come quickly and look." When we arrived, we could not see what you had just shown her. Excitedly she shared, as she pointed to a section of the sky, that she had just seen you dressed just as we envisage you in the Sacred Heart images. She never did stop loving you or following you, and on her death bed, you rewarded her with the blessings of the Nine First Fridays.

She had the comfort of the blessings of the Holy Roman Catholic Church that she had been faithful to all her life. As she received the last rights of the church from the hands of one of your Holy Roman Catholic Priests - it happened that one of her four sons was beside her during this anointing and he related the story as the priest himself did at her funeral, that just as he said the very last of the prayers of the anointing rights of the church - and anointed her forehead with the sign of the cross she took her last breath. Her son said, "I told the priest at the time that he must be a very powerful man to have it happen as it did."

But, I would like to thank you Jesus for fulfilling the promise you made to her as a young girl when she had taken it upon herself to ride her bike to the church every day on the first Friday of the month for nine months to show her love and trust in you. You most certainly did not let her down, showing her yourself in the sky before the cloud covered the vision, to being there at the hour of her death with what you had promised her - the last rights of the Holy Roman Catholic Church that she had followed you in all her life. Today, all I can say is thank you for your mercy My Lord and My God. Amen

I awoke one morning from a dream in which I was shown a Radio Station. I had no idea what this meant, so I asked the Lord in prayer.

My Prayer

Here I am Lord what is it you want me to receive?

Words Received

Below the line you will find your answer. They have pulled up roots and have moved their posts.

That is all; don't be fooled by the many smiles and acts of what is next for you. You continue to write and I will show you how much they want you to stop receiving.

My hand has been placed upon you and the Man in the Hat knows that you belong to me and he must remove himself and his hat, or I will do it for him.

Go in peace there is much for you to uncover.

I thank you Father God in Jesus Name. Amen.

11.
SHARE A MEMORY

I would like to share with you a memory that was awoken within me today as I read from the Catholic Voice. It was a message that our Archbishop gave reflecting on his upcoming trip to Rome, along with all the other Australian Bishops.

The formal name of the visit I am told is; Ad Limina Apostolorum

This literally means 'to the threshold of the Apostles.' – A visit to the tombs of St Peter and St Paul.

When I read this, my heart became soft and my mind went on the journey of remembering a vision I had been given over 24 years ago. I had been praying with a number of friends when it happened. I became aware that I was seeing the Holy Father; it was Saint, Pope John Paul II, and he was sitting on an old wooden chair surrounded by a circle of bishops or cardinals, I am not sure which. The Holy Father was just sitting there with his head down and no one was attempting to go to him or even offer a hand to help him, and he appeared to be so frail.

That part of the vision ceased, and now I found myself down under what I thought at the time was the crypt or burial chambers under the Vatican. Because I was now standing beside the tomb of St Peter and I began to shake it saying to St Peter as I desperately tried to unhinge the top of the tomb stone by shaking it vigorously; "Come up and help him, come up and help him." I said this because those who were gathered around the Holy Father were doing nothing to help him. At this point the vision ceased. After a while, as I began to reflect on what I had been shown, I shared the vision with others who were there.

As I have said it is over 24 years ago now, and the numbers of years I have been allotted to remain on this earth are known to God alone. So I don't mind if people don't believe me, when I tell them the things that God has shown to me.

My only concern is maybe that vision was given for this very time and to encourage us to pray, especially to Saint Peter, to come to help the Archbishop and all the Australian bishops who will visit at the tomb of St Peter.

Long ago, when I was given that vision I was unable to help, the now Saint, Pope John Paul II, I was just looking for someone to help him, I did not know who, or how I found myself at the tomb of St Peter, but I guess there was a special reason for it.

Since that time I have seen the Holy Father in a dream when he came accompanying one of my sisters who had also passed away. My sister came into a room where I was with a number of elderly people, and she was saying to me; "Get out of here you can do nothing for these elderly people, they have had their chance and they are in God's hands." With her was Saint, Pope John Paul II, but he just seemed to be accompanying her he did not speak, he was just there.

So many things come into my mind when I sit down to write my thoughts. I remembered again, walking into the Church at Goulburn during the time they were fixing the roof and found myself standing beside the two statues that had stood on the two corners of the Old Cathedral roof, but due to the restoration works were now standing on the church floor. Again I recall my attention being drawn to the rooster at St Peter's feet. This simple thing made a lasting impression upon me and I felt very close to St Peter and a little ashamed of my own denials of Jesus my Lord by not being brave enough to openly proclaim my Lord at all times.

May God have mercy on me, and may St Peter please pray for me.

Then I heard that one of the things that had survived the fire in the Cathedral of Notre Dame in France was the Rooster. It was seen toppling to the floor of the Cathedral during the fire. Could this have been another reminder by the Rooster of our failure to acknowledge Jesus Christ, as truly Lord and Saviour of the World?

If this is the faith that we profess, we should not be afraid to say it with all love, joy and peace, in our own hearts, knowing who it is we follow. While all the time respecting another's belief and not bombarding them with our own.

Jesus told the disciples when he sent them out, that if they were not welcomed in a town, to go out into the street and wipe the dust of that town from the soles of their shoes and leave that place. Once people have heard the Good News of Jesus Christ, it is then up to the person in regards to whether they want to become a follower of Jesus the Lord and accept him as their Lord and Saviour.

I guess this is really the message my sister was giving me in the dream – not to worry about those who know the word of God and keep it – but to worry about those who have heard the good news, but for some reason or another, have failed to hold onto it.

I say, be wary of such a person, for they can do you great harm with their own preconceived ideas. They will want to debate with you all that does not please them, as far as your faith goes.

Be loving and kind in such situations but, stand firm to the truth that you know in your heart regarding your loyalty to the One True and Holy God of the Trinity.

If they were to see the people of the God of the Trinity fulfilling Gods Commandments and living their lives accordingly - while proclaiming that Jesus Christ is Lord, I feel then, we would be seen as people of peace, who want to offer that same peace to all people of good will.

Words Received

The shining light of God's mercy has descended upon you Pam. He has been waiting for you to grow in confidence and to open your heart and mind to what you were created for. That is to give this message to the world and remember, that you will not be liked for doing so, for they have worked so hard to bring themselves to the position they are holding now in the community.

Open your computer and write what I say, so they may read it and know that I have seen all.

Go now - put the words I will give to you there and let them see.

Once you would not have been game enough to do this, but that time has now passed.

Go in peace.

12.
OUR LADY'S GROTTO

My Prayer

Here I am Lord what do you want me to say?

Words Received

My hand is upon the plough and the beasts of burden have begun to move in order to plough the soil.

It is time to get dressed with truth tied tightly around your waist, righteousness as your breast plate to keep out all the burning arrows shot by the evil one.

Wear on your feet eagerness to spread the good news of peace. Take the helmet of salvation and the word of God as the sword that the Spirit gives.

Pam, the soldiers have moved into position and they are circling My Holy House. Quickly tell my servant that he will be in the line of fire from their bullets. But I will send a defending Angel to keep him safe.

Are you ready to now finish writing what you were trying to - toward bringing the honour to my Mother?

I tell you many blessings will fall upon this parish and this place if true devotion is given to my holy Mother.

Go in peace and finish your letter.

My Letter to Holy Spirit Parish Council

Grotto to Our Lady

I had heard that consideration was being investigated to allow the building of a Grotto to Our Lady in the grounds of our church - so to express my gratitude to the council members, I forwarded the following letter.

'What a wonderful blessing it will be for all in the parish who have a great love and respect for the Holy Mother of Our Lord and Saviour Jesus Christ. We will be showing The Lord Jesus Christ her son, that his Mother is loved in this parish because she bought him our saviour into the world as God-man.

I am a woman in her seventies now who loves her Lord Jesus Christ with all her heart, but I believe in my inner being that is because his Holy Mother both protected me and led me to honour her beloved son. On many occasions during my life I found myself too timid to approach him myself so I would ask her to intercede for me.

I guess I am bearing my soul here because, after a while and to my embarrassment I became bolder in my requests and bypassed my wonderful Mother in asking for her help and guidance in all the best ways to honour and please her beloved son.

Overtime Our Lady, although, still my beloved mother was just there in the back ground somewhere. The joy and peace of knowing she was always there when I needed her became a little less over time although my faith and love for her and her beloved son never wavered. I somehow on looking back think things in my life began to become a little harder for me when she was not there.

Reflecting on so many things in regard to our blessed mother I am led to think about a comment I heard a priest say some years back and it has sprung to my mind this day. His comment on arriving home in Australia from overseas went something like this -

"I don't know why it is, but each time I arrive home and step off the plane, I feel as if I am stepping into a desert, after having experienced the faith, of the people I had just left. It was as if Australia was dry and lacking in something in this land."

I immediately thought on his words and wondered if it was the lack of the faith of the people to show honour to our Lady, especially when so many where expressing all sorts of reasons why we should not honour the Mother of our Lord Jesus Christ and the spouse of the Holy Spirit, especially as we are called the Land of the Holy Spirit.

If this is the case, then maybe many others like me may have slipped in showing our blessed Mother our love for her.

Again I would like to say a big thank you to the members of the Parish Pastoral Council for allowing such a wonderful gift to be given on behalf of The Holy Spirit Parish to Mary, the Mother of our Lord and Saviour, and to honour God the Holy Spirit the Third Person of the Trinity and spouse of Mary after whom our Parish is dedicated to.

13.

FEAST DAY OF ST PATRICK AND THE TRANSFIGURATION

My Prayer

Heavenly Father in the name of your beloved son, I come to seek your guidance and your help in understanding just what you want of me. I am so tired of the world and the worldly people who continue to push upon others their own way of thinking – telling us unless we follow their way of thinking then somehow we are not normal. I am not disputing what science has proven in any way for science is a great gift to your people Lord, and only foolish people would deny that – my concern is when people don't seem to be able to see that there is also a supernatural element at play in the spirit world also and that you God allow some to see and understand things that are not always explained by science.

The reason I no longer write much is because I have been told that this is not how the world thinks and that I should move away from my way of thinking. You know Lord, I don't care what they say, I just want to listen to you and write what I believe you allow me to hear.

Like at Mass this morning I had been feeling quite down, having remembered the words I had heard a short time back now at Mass that said, 'I know thee not'.

This morning I was speaking to Jesus in prayer, asking of him to explain what I could do to change things around so I could hear my Lord say, that, 'he knew me'.

Jesus my Lord and my saviour, I believe you heard my prayer at Mass this morning for as I returned to my seat I heard the words, 'I will never leave you.' Oh, what joy that bought to my heart and peace to my questioning mind.

Today is the feast day of St Patrick and although I am not Irish I am a fifth generation Australian of ancestors who did come from Irish and English backgrounds.

Today I felt a great desire to recognise this at Mass this morning and I offered my Holy Communion for my ancestors who so long ago came to Australia – some in chains others as free citizens. It must have been a very hard and strange land for them but they persevered in their efforts to survive in its different climate to what they had left behind in Ireland and England.

Now, I am home after Mass and I have taken up the Church bulletin to read; one of the first things I see is the children's cartoon drawing under the heading Transfiguration and the caption reads, 'This is my Son the Beloved, listen to Him'. Then I glanced to see the words 'Pause for thought - The Transfiguration' - beside it. So I did pause for thought.

I had no hesitation about how wonderful the mountain top experience might have been for Peter, James, and John, as they witnessed the wonderful dazzling white of Jesus clothes.

I would like to share something that happened to my sister and I back in the 1990s. My sister was visiting me from my old home town of Boorowa for the day. She had a great devotion and love for Our Lady and she had also heard about the statue that our Parish Priest had placed in the grounds beside the church in Goulburn where I was living at the time. As I recall, Father had dedicated the statue under the title 'Our Lady Protector of Families', as it was the year of the family.

My sister asked if it would be possible for us to go and visit the statue before she went home. It was still quite sunny in the afternoon when we arrived there. My sister became so excited when she seen the statue and began to say things like; Oh she is beautiful as she lovingly stroked our Lady's hand.

Now we were standing side by side in front of the statue just looking lovingly at it and remembering we were honouring our Lady by showing reverence before it.

It was at this point that something so wonderful happened that it took my breath away. The statue was white in colour; no other colour on it, just all white – but suddenly the colour became a shade whiter and seeing it my breath took another gasp - but directly following the first colour of the statue growing whiter, it did it again and again. Three times in all until the statue was whiter than anything one could imagine or anyone could paint it. It was on the third gasp for air from me, that the statue returned to being perfectly normal.

I looked at my sister and she at me, and all we could say was, "Did you see that"? "*Yes*"! We both had seen the statue transformed into three different dazzling shades of white before returning to normal. We were both so delighted to have witnessed such an event – I believe in my heart that it was given to us in order to help us both through trying times that was to lay before us on our journey of life.

Our Lady showed us her love for her family that day, as she held the baby Jesus in her arms before her in the statue. I think about this and how the family has come under such attack from Satan and his cohorts since that day - the day when we stood together before our blessed Mother there in Goulburn, and witnessed this great blessing.

I don't talk about this much anymore, for I see the negative reaction that surrounds my explanation of the event. The last time I shared this story with someone they said, "I guess that is something you would not forget, but I would have to see it to believe it".

All this happened such a long time ago now and my sister has been dead for many years also.

May she rest in peace. Amen

Funny how certain things prompt ones memory as you get older and this little cartoon drawing on today's bulletin has led me to remember just some of the things that God has done and continues to do in my life to show me his presence and love.

Today it was the words I started with that I heard after Holy Communion, 'I will never leave you'.

As I journeyed on through the bulletin I came across the story relating to St Patrick's life – he being born in Britain - and captured by Irish pirates and sold into slavery. Spending six years in Ireland before escaping and returning to his family where he trained for the priesthood before God returned him to Ireland. I love the legend about St Patrick and his banishing of all snakes from Ireland.

Then I read St Patricks Breastplate Prayer - which I believed was written by him in 433A.D. for divine protection.

Here, I think of Ephesians Chapter: 6 where we are told to put on the whole Armour of God. I wonder how many of us rush into a new day and run headlong into the storms that come against us, and have failed to dress ourselves with the protection of Our Lord. Everyday can be a battle against the enemy and the worldly people, and we need to be true soldiers in our Lords army dressed and ready for battle if we want to survive.

So as true Christians in the army of Jesus Christ of our Lord and Saviour - let us put on the Armour of the Lord and stand ready – with truth tired tightly around our waist, with righteousness as our breastplate, and on our feet eagerness to proclaim the Good News of peace. While carrying faith as a shield, to put out all the burning arrows shot by the Evil One. Let us accept salvation as our helmet, and the word of God as the sword which the Spirit gives us.

We are reminded in Holy Scripture to do all this in prayer, asking for Gods help. Praying on every occasion, as the Spirit leads.

I feel this is what St Patrick was saying, when he said that when Christ goes with us, we are well defended on every side. And we should not be afraid for we know who it is that walks with us.

And that brings me back to the wonderful words I heard at Mass this morning.

I Will Never Leave You.

14.
THE PROPHET JOB

Words Received

Believe in me Pam for the angel is already busy rewriting my reply to you and to the whole world.

My hand has been extended over those who have caused you so much misery. Their names have been recorded and they will not be forgotten.

Holy you must now become – not just holy in isolation – but holy before the world.

Angels this day are recruiting my people to come follow you.

Remain firm in your stance and watch them move away. For they will see that you cannot be removed from the road I have placed you on.

Open my Holy Word at Job 19 – My hand is always upon those who love me and listen to my word.

Go in peace.

Job 19: 1-29

Why do you keep tormenting me with words?

Time after time you insult me and show no shame for the way you abuse me.

Even if I have done wrong, how does that hurt you?

You think you are better than I am, and regard my troubles as proof of my guilt.

Can't you see it is God who has done this? He has set a trap to catch me.

I protest against his violence, but no one is listening; no one hears my cry for justice.

God has blocked the way, and I can't get through; he has hidden my path in darkness.

He has taken away all my wealth and destroyed my reputation.

He batters me from every side. He uproots my hope and leaves me to wither and die.

God is angry and rages against me; he treats me like his worst enemy.

He sends his army to attack me; they dig trenches and lay siege to my tent.

God has made my own family forsake me; I am a stranger to those who knew me; my relatives and friends are gone.

Those who were guests in my house have forgotten me; my servant women treat me like a stranger and a foreigner.

When I call a servant, he doesn't answer –

Even when I beg him to help me.

My wife can't stand the smell of my breath, and my own brothers won't come near me.

Children despise me and laugh when they see me.

My closest friends look at me with disgust; those I loved most have turned against me.

My skin hangs loose on my bones; I have barely escaped with my life.

You are my friends! Take pity on me! The hand of God has struck me down.

Why must you persecute me the way God does? Haven't you tormented me enough?

How I wish that someone would remember my words and record them in a book!

Or with a chisel carve my words in stone and write them so that they would last forever.'

But I know there is someone in heaven who will come at last to my defence.

Even after my skin is eaten by disease while still in this body I will see God.

I will see him with my own eyes, and he will not be a stranger.

My courage failed because you said,

'How can we torment him?' You looked for some excuse to attack me.

But now, be afraid of the sword -----

The sword that brings God's wrath on sin, so that you will know there is one who judges.

15.

ISAIAH: THE EVIL THAT PEOPLE DO

I was also encouraged to read the prophet Isaiah.

Isaiah 5: 8-25

You are doomed! You buy more houses and land to add to what you already have. Soon there will be nowhere for anyone else to live, and you alone will live in the land.

I have heard the Lord Almighty say, "All these big, fine houses will be empty ruins.

The grapevines growing on two hectares of land will yield only twenty litres of wine. Ten bags of seed will produce only one bag of grain."

You are doomed! You get up early in the morning to start drinking, and you spend long evenings getting drunk.

At your feasts you have harps and tambourines and flutes – and wine. But you don't understand what the Lord is doing, and so you will be carried away as prisoners. Your leaders will starve to death, and the common people will die of thirst.

The world of the dead is hungry for them, and it opens its mouth wide. It gulps down the nobles of Jerusalem along with the noisy crowd of common people.

Everyone will be disgraced, and all who are proud will be humbled.

But the Lord Almighty shows his greatness by doing what is right, and he reveals his holiness by judging his people.

In the ruins of the cities lambs will eat grass and young goats will find pasture.

You are doomed! You are unable to break free from your sins.

You say, "Let the Lord hurry up and do what he says he will, so that we can see it. Let Israel's holy God carry out his plans; let's see what he has in mind."

You are doomed! You call evil good and call good evil. You turn darkness into light and light into darkness. You make what is bitter sweet, and what is sweet you make bitter.

You are doomed! You think you are wise, so very clever.

You are doomed! Heroes of the wine bottle! Brave and fearless when it comes to mixing drinks!

But for just a bribe you let the guilty go free, and you prevent the innocent from getting justice.

So now, just as straw and dry grass shrivel and burn in the fire, your roots will rot and your blossoms will dry up and blow away, because you have rejected what the Lord Almighty, Israel's holy God, has taught us.

The Lord is angry with his people and has stretched out his hand to punish them. The mountains will shake, and the bodies of those who die will be left in the streets like rubbish. Yet even then the Lord's anger will not be ended, but his hand will still be stretched out to punish.

God Calls Isaiah to Be a Prophet Chapter: 6: 1-13

In the year that King Uzziah died, I saw the Lord. He was sitting on his throne, high and exalted, and his robe filled the whole Temple.

Around him flaming creatures were standing, each of which had six wings. Each creature covered its face with two wings, and its body with two, and used the other two for flying.

They were calling out to each other:

"Holy, holy, holy!

The Lord Almighty is holy!

His glory fills the world."

The sound of their voices made the foundation of the Temple shake, and the Temple itself was filled with smoke.

I said, "There is no hope for me! I am doomed because every word that passes my lips is sinful, and I live among a people whose every word is sinful. And yet, with my own eyes I have seen the King, the Lord Almighty."

Then one of the creatures flew down to me, carrying a burning coal that he had taken from the altar with a pair of tongs.

He touched my lips with the burning coal and said, "This has touched your lips, and now your guilt is gone, and your sins are forgiven."

Then I heard the Lord say, "Who shall I send? Who will be our messenger?" I answered, "I will go! Send me!"

So he told me to go and give the people this message: "No matter how much you listen, you will not understand. No matter how much you look, you will not know what is happening."

Then he said to me, "Make the minds of these people dull, their ears deaf, and their eyes blind, so that they cannot see or hear or understand. If they did, they might turn to me and be healed."

I asked, "How long will it be like this, Lord?"

He answered, "Until the cities are ruined and empty – until the houses are uninhabited – until the land itself is a desolate wasteland.

I will send the people far away and make the whole land desolate.

Even if one person out of ten remains in the land, he too will be destroyed; he will be like the stump of an oak tree that has been cut down."

The Lord Warns The Prophet. Chapter: 8:11-15

With his great power the Lord warned me not to follow the path which the people were following. He said, "Do not join in the schemes of the people and do not be afraid of the things that they fear.

Remember that I, the Lord Almighty, am holy; I am the one you must fear.

Because of my awesome holiness I am like a stone that people stumble over; I am like a trap that will catch the people of the kingdoms of Judah and Israel and the people of Jerusalem.

Many will stumble; they will fall and be crushed. They will be caught in a trap."

16.
GOOD MORNING LORD

My Prayer

Good morning Lord, thank you for bringing into being this new day. Thank you for bringing me into this new day. I call to the trinity the One True and Holy God for mercy, help and direction, and a right attitude in knowing how to approach my life today – so many secrets so many unanswered questions – so much done behind my back that has made me doubt so many. Please forgive me, and help me to do what is right in your sight. In the name of Jesus your beloved son, I seek the answers – asking in His Name for His Glory. Amen.

Words Received

Come home, we are waiting for you to return to the land of your birth. Those who deceived you and caused you so much pain have departed. They have run their race and now will be no longer able to imprison you, or the thoughts that

I place within you. Many now know the truth – that truth will set you free, and in that freedom you will bring forth the wisdom that they searched for but were unable to receive. The healing hand of your God has been placed upon you both – that one has been greatly deceived by the enemy – but has come to understand that man cannot live by bread alone, but indeed need the manner that only God can give. They have been spending all their wisdom in order to market the fruits and spoils of the earth to gain the money they so worship.

Come now, I am giving you the opening into this new life and it will be one lit by my lamp, the flame of the Spirit. You have decided that enough has been enough, and for this I commend you. For you needed to come to this point in order to bring freedom and wisdom to others also.

Why do you think I allowed you to carry on as I did? It was to allow you to gain the confidence and the wisdom that has been growing within you. My beloved is mine and I am hers and my banner over her is love. Love to give, love to share that will bring into being a million smiles from hearts set free from the imprisonment that they are all in, not game to open their mouths, for if they do, they know that others will expose them. They have made themselves into secret tribes and have used as their mascot the platypus. The secret and hard to find animal, which holds many different parts upon its body in order to make it look like not just one group.

Believe Pam in me, and in the one I sent. We are coming to bring into your life the necessary gifts that you will need to help the many. Are you ready? -

Yes Lord, I am ready - May your glory be shown in what you do Lord. Amen.

My Prayer

I offer my day into your hands Lord - whatever I do, or say may it only be in accordance with your will to bring healing to those around me and to myself also. Please don't let me fall into temptation and sin this day. May my holy guardian angel and my special helpers, continue to help and guide me and my loved ones, protecting us from all injury, accident, sickness, and deadly diseases and from the evil one. I give my thanks to you my Father in Heaven, in and by the name of your only beloved son Jesus Christ my Lord, and my saviour. Amen.

Words Received

The healing hand of my son is being placed upon you and your house hold. Never again will they be led down such a path of destruction. Never will so many be fooled again Pam. They were like children let loose in a candy store and the enemy feed them various amounts of sugar to make it all seem so exciting and real. He never once tried to stop the gravy train running at full speed, because he knew it would eventually crash and they would all be expelled, and when that happened their sorrow would be great and their anger even greater.

The healing hand of your God is all that will help people to come to understand just what this train wreck will cause on the whole world.

Believe Pam; just continue to believe in me and in the one I sent. He will allow you to receive from my hands all that I tell him, just as he did when he walked upon the earth. He told the people in obedience to me, all that I told him to say. Believe in him and give him the glory for what he has done for you and your loved ones. He is my beloved son, the one in whom I am well pleased.

Many years ago he heard your prayer to show you his father and that prayer reached my heart from his hands, and so you were greatly privileged to have been shown the Father by the hands of the Son. Be happy this day, all is in readiness for you to move away from the mess and to start a new beginning with all your loved ones. Go in peace to love and to serve your God.

My Prayer

Don't know what to say Father God this morning, not feeling very well. I can only hope for your mercy and protection in Jesus name. Amen.

Words Received

Believe Pam, just believe, you do not know it yet but you have won the race. Many are in turmoil this day wondering just what has gone wrong with their clever plans to change the world. Go in peace and enjoy this day.

Thank you Father God. Amen.

My Prayer

My Lord and my God

Behold the handmaid of the Lord. Be it done unto me according to your word.

Lord, I started to write my prayer but just out of the blue, the words that our Lady uttered in the Magnificat came flooding into my mind; so I wrote them down in honour of Our Lady, when she accepted the Archangel Gabriel's visit to be the mother of our saviour. Amen

Thank you Blessed Mother for your obedience to God. I don't know what to say here, so I will just ask if there is anything for me to write. My mind is very slow this morning, I feel as if the world is running so fast with so many people in prominent positions unable to take control of the chaos - is this the runaway train that Satan put so many people on. Oh, please tell me what if anything I can do to help bring about peace. Amen

Words Received

The healing hand of Jesus will never leave those who call for his help. My beloved, you are under a state of anxiety this day, but if you open your Bible you will read there my love and direction for your day. Are you ready? Yes Lord, just allow me to do as you say.

Why were you born? Why were you born at all? So many people are asking this at this time – believing that what they are or who they have become, has made no help at all to the world I created. But they are wrong, and when they are called home into my heavenly presence they will see where their lives have taken them and the people, the good and the bad, that they came across in their life to make it better or worse for them.

Open my Holy Word at Mark 16:

An Old Ending to The Gospel.

Jesus appears to Mary Magdalene - Mark 16: 9-11

After Jesus rose from death early on Sunday, he appeared first to Mary Magdalene, from whom he had driven out seven demons. She went and told his companions. They were mourning and crying; and when they heard her say that Jesus was alive and that she had seen him, *they did not believe her.*

Jesus appears to two followers - Mark 16: 12-13

After this, Jesus appears in a different manner to two of them while they were on their way to the country. They returned and told the others, *but they would not believe.*

Jesus appears to the Eleven – Mark 16: 14-18

Last of all, Jesus appears to the eleven disciples as they were eating. He scolded them, because they did not have faith and because they were too stubborn to believe those who had seen him alive. He said to them, "Go throughout the whole world and preach the gospel to all people. Whoever *believes* and is baptised will be saved; whoever does not *believe* will be condemned. *Believers* will be given the power to perform miracles, they will drive out demons in my name, they will speak in strange tongues, if they pick up snakes or drink any poison, they will not be harmed, they will place their hands on sick people, and they will get well".

Jesus is taken up to Heaven - Mark 16: 19-20

After the Lord Jesus had talked with them, he was taken up to heaven and sat at the right hand side of God. The disciples went and preached everywhere, and the Lord worked with them and proved that their preaching was true by the miracles that were performed.

Another Old Ending Mark 16: 9-10

The women went to Peter and his friends and gave them a brief account of all they had been told. After this, Jesus himself sent out through his disciples, from the east to the west, the sacred and ever *living message of eternal salvation.*

My Prayer

Good morning Lord, thank you and praise you for your great mercy. Amen.

Words Received

You will open my word and there you will find your answer. My name, the name above all names will rise up to show you what you must do. Go now, be open to my prompting and remain open until you find your answer. I know you are feeling that you don't know where to look, so I will allow you to remain in this state until you obey me by just opening and reading my word. Heal the sick, and remember that there are more-sick now than ever.

Go in peace.

Matthew 11:25-30

Come to Me and Rest

At that time Jesus said, "Father, Lord of heaven and earth! I thank you because you have shown to the unlearned what you have hidden from the wise and learned. Yes, Father, this was how you wanted it to happen.

"My Father has given me all things. No one knows the Son except the Father, and no one knows the Father except the Son and those to whom the Son chooses to reveal him.

"Come to me, all of you who are tired from carrying heavy loads and I will give you rest. Take my yoke and put it on you, and learn from me, because I am gentle and humble in spirit; and you will find rest. For the yoke I will give you is easy, and the load I put on you is light".

My Prayer

Good morning Father God, thank you for your faithfulness in bringing in this new day. Thank you for bringing me also into this day - I know not what I should do for my heart and spirit are both in a place I would sooner not be, for it is making my heart feel angry and not wanting to know any-more. No matter what I do, I feel it will not be enough to rectify the situation and all the time I have been trying, I find I am not using the gifts that the Spirit of God gave to me out of fear. If I write something then others will just take and use it according to their will, and I will have no say or control over it.

Many times I have thought of just walking away and leaving it all to them, but something keeps stirring me up and I just have to continue on. I don't know if it is pride or anger on my part, but it really does hurt to know that so many deceived me. Please have mercy on me for my anger.

I am trying to let go and allow the anger to subside so that all those that I have sent my anger against, will also be free from my anger against them. Once it would not have been so hard, but the longer it goes on the harder it is becoming. Please forgive me Lord Jesus – for it really is affecting my health and I don't know what I should do?

Words Received

Pam, if you are sincere and you really want healing, well then ask and you will receive. Why wait any longer for others to help you when you have the Lord himself by your side. Do you think he is not watching all that is happening? Do you imagine you are on your own through all of this? No child, there have been many who used you. But there have been others who truly wanted to help you. My advice is for you to seek out the truth of those that wanted to help but were unable to do so because they would have exposed themselves to others who would not have understood their situation. Believe Pam, for your words have given comfort to many, so continue on, the day will come when all will be revealed. Go in peace to start your day.

I thank you Father, Son, and Holy Spirit. Amen

My Prayer

Good morning Father God, you know the state of my mind and my health this day. I have just read where you told me some time back, you would leave me in this state until I obeyed you by just opening and reading your word. You also said, heal the sick, and to remember that there are more-sick now than ever before.

Lord, I have been trying to do your will be it ever so badly - but I feel as if there is no end to the words and places where my ID has not be compromised. What should I do, please tell me? I seek your wisdom to know how to approach it all. In the name of Jesus please clear the path for all to walk safely upon it into your anointing presence. Amen.

Words Received

The time for the renewal of My Holy Catholic Church has arrived. I have allowed it to be cleansed of many who had no right to be there in the first place. You have only seen a remnant of those that were placing upon the shoulders of my holy men and women in order to make them stumble and fall. Many where delighting in the actions they were involved with - thinking that they were completely in control. Many made much money on their way to standing tall in their community, but it was all for nothing, for their ivory towers that they built are falling around them like a ton of bricks.

My daughter, don't give up, remove all and they will real-ise that it has come to an end. You have heard the anger in other voices for they were sure they were right.

My Prayer

Holy Father God, may your name be praised and glorified forever. I come to do your will Lord, please assist me in my efforts in Jesus mighty name I make my prayer. Amen

Words Received

The Spirit of the Lord says, Come, come my child and open your heart to receive all that I have to give to you. I am asking you this day to come closer and open your mind afresh to all that you already know. Show the children of the poor that there are many who are poorer than those who suffer insuffi-cient food and clothing. There are those whose spirit knows me not. They are in a far worst place than the first poor, for the day will come when they will stand before me and will know me not. What a sad day for them for although they had every opportunity to come follow me, they made no attempt to do so.

Pam, not all who are in the dark are there because they have not heard, I tell you they are there because it has been their own decision to go there and stay there. The blind that are deprived of the light for their eyes to see can in many cases see more clearly than those who have eyes to see.

Child, you are unsure of many things but remember this:

Show mercy where mercy is needed. Show love where love is needed and show hope where hope is needed.

Go in peace.

My Prayer after Morning Mass

Good morning Lord, I come to do your will. I want to finish writing the words for this book - please tell me if this is the right thing to do? I make my prayer in Jesus name. Amen

Words Received

You have been waiting for so long and now the time for you to come follow me in the real world has arrived. All you have to do is be true to yourself and your own feelings. They will lead you into a positive position that will bring anointing to your life and to the lives of many.

By your hand you will see the blind see, the dumb speak, and the deaf hear. Are you able to cope with this?

Yes Lord, let your will be done. You alone are my Lord and Savour and you alone send who you want and to where and how you want them to go.

Angels have gathered here Pam, and now you must do your part.

Yes, put your words together and finish the book and this is what I will use to open the floodgates of heaven to bring about healing and peace for all.

Go now, no time to waste.

My Prayer

Good morning Lord all glory honour and praise to your most Holy Name.

Once I was lost but now I'm found

Once I was lost now I'm free

Once I was bound and unable to walk

Once I was timid but now that's gone

Once I was silent but now no more

Once I was lonely but not now

Once I left home to begin a new life

Once I found my new life I became me

What a silly thing to write Lord, but they were words flowing into my mind and I liked what they could represent. A new beginning from the life I have left behind by your grace and mercy.

Why do I feel this is necessary this morning Father God? I can only hope and pray that all that has taken place is finished, and in that final chapter, I am also free along with all my family.

May each of us be able to live freely, peacefully and in good health. And grow each day in our love for you both in our words, and in our actions. In Jesus name Father God I pray. Amen

Words Received

The leading hand has been removed Pam and now you do not have to follow. My hand is the only hand now that will lead you. Your mission has finished and it was a long journey. Those who encroached around you and suffocated your works will find no comfort as they look back upon their actions, for they will see all was for naught.

Daughter, if you are serious you will be able to make that new start into your life this day and I will watch over you and bless you in all you do. My world waits what you will do now; it is the time of my blessing. You can freely rejoice and freely live the life you have missed out on, as you studied that which I wanted to show you.

Dangling from that tree that so many hung their hats on, was not the tree for you. You were well and wise to have avoided that page in your life. Go daughter and enjoy your day.

Thank you my Lord and my God.

My Prayer

Good morning Lord how wonderful to have lived to see another morning here on your beautiful earth. Thank you and all praise and glory to you my wonderful God. How I love the Most Holy Trinity, the Father who created me, the Son who saved me, and the Holy Spirit who guides me. Three divine persons - in the one true and Holy God of the Trinity. Amen.

For some reason the names of your holy people who have played parts in my life came into my mind. Especially the three people you once told me would help me in my life's journey. These three I thank you for, and I am sorry that I have not become closer to them. I hope they and you will forgive me for that and help me to rectify it - the others without saying, your Blessed Mother and Saint Joseph her spouse. And one who has meant a lot to me and I have asked if he would pray for me if he was in a position to do so – that being the Prophet Jeremiah of the Old Testament.

Father, today after all I read yesterday about Aussie towns really made me very sad, but in another sense very sure that everything you had told me was true. Remembering some of those things hurts a lot, for I had been hoping that it had not been so. Thank you for keeping me in the (not so sure place) for so long or I might not have been able to stay the distance. But now that I know, I hope and pray that you will return those two places, as you said you would, back to those who really love you and are still living in them.

My Lord and My God, I went back and read what had been written yesterday and I guess it answered all for me. Maybe, just maybe it might have been better not to know! I will leave it for you to decide for me my Father God. Amen.

My Prayer

Come Holy Spirit you are so very welcome in my life - all glory to your name. Amen.

Words Received

All those who used us for their own profile, will no longer be able to do so. Pam, even your closest friend sat silent beside you while observing everything that was happening.

My Prayer

Lord, I don't know if it is too late to ask if you want me to listen and write but here I am Lord if you do. I want so much to return to you – knowing in my heart that everything will be all right – but you know my thoughts – my doubts – there have been too many secrets for me to feel comfortable anymore. I wish I could escape from the doubts that enter my mind.

I put them into your hands this day Father God and in the name of your beloved Son I seek your help and your mercy - Is there no place left on this earth for me to be my own person. It is a terrible thing to be in bondage by others, especially when there are no physical signs to show that you are. It wears you down overtime and I know this for a fact. You just give up because you can't escape the secret actions of others and have no proof to confront them with. They are scot-free and they know it. What would you do Lord?

Words Received

My child, I would delight in what awaits you. You know not the time or the place when your freedom will occur. Try not to hurry to the end Pam, for in between there will be a time of joy. You will understand later this day that even though so many rode the wave of hope and prosperity under much that I had given to you, their wave has come crashing into the shore and them with it. What fools they look even though they don't want to admit it.

You continue on as led by My Spirit and I will bring about much healing for your heart and peace for your mind. For it is coming a time, when the wave they rode to the shore will greatly recede and begin to pull them back into the ocean, only this time, it will be for them alone to try and survive by their own strength. Many will come to understand that before when they were taking my words and using them to make themselves look good – now it will be by their own strength that they will have to survive. Go in peace, I will show you new things this day.

Words Received

Believe in the Trinity Pam don't let anyone tell you differently. I the Lord your God has given you the ability to look and see many things that other eyes cannot see. Rejoice in this knowledge, for it will bring comfort to your own heart. Yes, many are wondering about their future this day and by morning many others will also be wondering – only to realise that no matter what they do to try and bring about their own agenda, it will not happen.

Believe my child, that, what you hear me say is to bring comfort to your own heart and soul. Many have commissioned themselves into a position that was not theirs to occupy only now are they realising how unsure that position is that they have put themselves into.

Go now and believe that before this day has passed many will be exposed for the serious nonsense that they have created simply believing that their own knowledge would bring them to the wealth that they were seeking.

Believe my daughter, believe all that I have told you and then you will be free to follow me in peace and joy. Allow those who have loved you, bring about that peace and joy. Open your heart to your loved ones and allow many to understand that my mercy is great to anyone who finds true repentance in their hearts - go in peace.

My Prayer

My Lord and My God thank you for this day – may your name be honoured and praised forever. Amen.

Words Received

The mighty hand of your God has been extended Pam and now the few that had been involved in bringing about many disasters for some - will no longer be able to spread the lies that so easily flowed from the lips.

Show yourself to those who would rather you did not and allow them to see that what I am saying is about to happen. They can plan and they can lie, but there is nothing they can do to stop the disaster that is about to hit their lives. You wonder what that could be, but it is not for you to know as yet. I will give you warning and when that warning comes you too, must gather your belongings and retreat to a safer place. Allow no one to put doubts into your mind regarding what I am telling you, and then you will be safe.

The crimes that have been committed are too much for me to overlook - and therefore my hand, the hand of God must intervene for the sake of the just. For if I don't, even the just will lose heart and become part of the flock of the unruly.

Why do you think I have waited so long before making my move to act? Child, there are many people who are trying to follow me as they know how - and for their sake, I have remained aloof in order for the unjust to repent. Some have, and that is good but, those who are in high places and hold the keys to the treasury have failed to hear the cry of the poor - but I have, and their day of atonement is coming quickly.

My Prayer

Holy God, Holy Mighty One, to you alone be the glory. May your name be praised and honored forever.

In the name of Jesus the beloved son, I make this prayer. Amen.

Words Received

The healing hand of God needs to be laid upon my people Pam, but they will not listen. They have gathered together to bring their own healing and forgiveness. But they cannot turn away from the road that leads to destruction. All have wandered away from my holy ways. Only a few have remained - someone told them that they had good ideas on how to bring about wealth and prosperity and so many just jumped up to follow with no regards as to what they were leaving in order to follow this dream.

A dream is all that it was. There was no revival, just a man-made project to resemble a revival.

Child, there will be a revival, but one that will be God made and led by My Holy Spirit and then those who come to follow me will not leave as you have seen in the past.

Pam, today there will be a big decision for you to make and I ask you to think about it clearly, for the wrong answer could put you in a terrible place.

Ask the Lord to show you the right place and you will not go wrong.

Please Lord Jesus Christ, please show me the right place; do not leave me to make this decision, because I may take the wrong path – please, please don't let me make the wrong choice.

You will remain in the place where I am now about to lead you to and there you will find rest for your soul.

Come, open my word and read Jeremiah Chapter 24: and remember I am with you always.

Go in peace. Amen.

Jeremiah Chapter 24:

Two Baskets of Figs

The Lord showed me two baskets of figs placed in front of the Temple. (This was after King Nebuchadnezzar of Babylonia had taken away Jehoiakim's son, King Jehoiachin of Judah, as a prisoner from Jerusalem to Babylonia, together with the leaders of Judah, the craft workers, and the skilled workers.) The first basket contained good figs, those that ripen early; the other one contained bad figs, too bad to eat. Then the Lord said to me, "Jeremiah, what do you see?"

I answered "Figs. The good ones are very good, and the bad ones are very bad, too bad to eat."

So the Lord said to me, "I, the Lord, the God of Israel, consider that the people who were taken away to Babylonia are like these good figs, and I will treat them with kindness. I will watch over them and bring them back to this land. I will build them up and not tear them down; I will plant them and not pull them up. I will give them the desire to know that I am the Lord. Then they will be my people, and I will be their God, because they will return to me with all their heart.

"As for King Zedekiah of Judah, the politicians around him, and the rest of the people of Jerusalem who have stayed in this land or moved to Egypt - I, the Lord, will treat them all like these figs that are too bad to be eaten. I will bring such a disaster on them that all the nations of the world will be terrified. People will make fun of them, make jokes about them, ridicule them, and use their name as a curse everywhere I scatter them. I will bring war, starvation, and disease on them until there is not one of them left in the land that I gave to them and their ancestors."

17.
BELIEVE, JUST BELIEVE

My Prayer

Heavenly Father, what are we becoming? Some of our politicians behave as if they have nothing to fear in their outrageous actions, and to some of us who have no way of expressing our feelings about things for we are too small in the eyes of the world, and there are already so many different voices yelling their opinions already - that no one would be able to hear anything we wanted to say anyway.

Yet they just go on in many cases not speaking the truth. From one who watches from the outside, it comes as a great sadness as I watch some of these people in power who say they love and serve you, all the time are seeking just more wealth and more power.

My Dream

I had a dream last night in which I was in a church. I won't say where the church was, but it appeared the people were getting ready for something. In the dream, I made my way to the back of the church after having been to confession.

I returned to my seat where a nun had been kneeling praying but was now gone. I started my prayers. A priest came along and said something like, "Those who have done the course, we are ready to start now". I replied, "I don't know what to do, as I have not done the course". I thought he would just tell me what to do and I would be able to participate, but instead he told me to leave, and so I did.

I went outside and made my way to a side door of the church and re-entered there. I thought I could just sit there with some other people and watch what was to happen. But now I found that there was no chairs free, so I had to go looking for one – at that time I woke from my dream.

Whatever the reason - I had a distinct feeling that I had been driven out of the work being put together to honor you in your holy house.

That, my Father is my thoughts that have come my way this morning and I wonder if there is anything you wish me to write. Amen.

Words Received

The believer will bring about much change Pam. The one who knows me, just because they know and love me will be given much grace and much power. Those that you speak about may know about me, may believe they love me, and may find in their heart a small spark that could be ignited if only they were game enough to move away from the group that holds so many of them in bondage. Tell your loved ones to bring into being all that they know in their hearts that is true. They have witnessed your life and they know what I have shown you is true and they know how powerful my words are.

Do not be anxious for others, just be anxious for yourself and remain always under my protection while the world cruises into its own disaster, for disaster is what will happen.

They believe disaster will not happen; but just like those at the Tower of Babel they will watch as their plans fail, their towers crumble and those that don't crumble, will just stand like statues on the landscape, for no one will be able to buy them.

Believe Pam; just believe, for I am giving you this message so you can share it with others who will benefit from hearing it.

You are wondering about your book and if it will ever be finished, Child, the book is almost completed and it is with my words from your pen. Be happy to witness what I will do with it.

Go in peace.

Words Received

Believe Pam, just believe and I will show you more than you can ever imagine. Dine in my presence and receive the reward that awaits you. Before you were born my hand embraced you, and I knew you would be my beloved daughter.

Holy I Am, and holy all people must become if they want to know me. You must understand that the enemy has been feeding my people with lies for so long that no one can tell the difference now between a lie and the truth. How sad for those who truly want to walk in the light – but because of the darkness are unable to find it.

Child so many have gone into the dark believing that the light of Christ would follow and protect them there. Where in my Holy Word were such words recorded?

I believe you and many like you will come to understand, how blessed you have been to have been shielded from such non-sense. Those who tried to destroy my Holy House will come to realise that their efforts have been in vain. I will show the true believers that only when they stand up for themselves in following me and return to the proper place of worship, will they receive the blessings they are seeking. They cry out in their woes saying 'Why am I left to battle all alone.' Showing no thought that they are living in the dark among dark people like themselves, engulfed - with no light - but continuing to walk blindly behind the one that says, 'Come follow me further into the darkness.'

Jesus my beloved son invited them to come follow him into the light, but they rejected him for the darkness and soon, very soon, the darkness will cover the earth.

Oh, there will be light just as today from the sun, but the darkness I speak about is the darkness of Satan. The hate, the lies, the destruction, and all the evil you see upon your television screens is what they are walking into and once they are there, they will become like refugees caught in makeshift camps, relying upon others generosity to feed them and protect them. So many young and old have walked this path and found no end to their journey.

Will you tell my people not all that call me Lord will enter the kingdom of heaven as so many believe it is their given right to do so. Angels and Saints may sing in their midst – but each person must be responsible for their own actions thoughts and deeds.

Why am I saying this Pam? Because you need to know that the decision you made to come follow me means just that.

You will be shown a new path to enable you to walk more easily upon for you to fulfill my will. I have a plan for many and that plan also includes you. Join my holy people and walk with faith into this new land where darkness cannot and will not be able to enter.

Are you ready to come follow me where ever I will lead you?

You know I will do my best to do so Father God. Amen.

My Prayer

Good morning Father God, thank you for bringing into being this new day and for allowing me to live to see it.

Father God, as I write this I am reminded again of the old movie I spoke about at the beginning of this book, and I am amazed at the similarity of the lives lived between the characters in that story and mine. In regards to how for years, the novice nun's place was kept by our wonderful Lady The Blessed Mother, and no one knew that the young nun was not in her rightful place.

Looking back upon my own life I can see that I too was there but unbeknownst to many, except for a few who knew that God had called me the Obedient One.

In this way, I walked about each day among the people unnoticed, isolated from the world around me. How I had hoped to be included in the many activities I could see being put in place to bring the message of the Holy Son of God Most High into the world. But so little were the invitations that came and even fewer to ask what I thought.

How sad my life became, because you were my life, all I had wanted to do was to serve you and honor you and to be part of your people, but alas, I was not wanted and not known for the gift you had given to me. Believe me Father God when I say it was not easy being so shunned – but if it was your will, then so be it. That is why today, I would like to put these few words together to tell the world of my love for you and your beloved son, and for your Holy Roman Catholic Church.

Many years have come and gone since I started to hear your words, and many have been used by others to help spread your love and peace. I pray that even though it was unbeknown to me, I pray that the words gave some people your hope and your mercy to encourage them.

You often tell me to believe, well my Lord and my God, I do believe, I believe that you and you alone are the Holy One; I believe that Jesus Christ is your only beloved son, and I believe in your Holy Spirit. Yes Father with all my heart I believe in the Trinity, I believe that in the three persons of the Trinity there is only one God to whom I give all the glory for writing these words.

Words Received

Show yourself to the priests and allow them to repair the damage that has been caused. They are my Holy Men who have been set aside to bring my message of hope for eternal life to many. Pam, are you ready to trust them – because my daughter you should.

Go in peace.

My Reflections for this day:

Today like many days when I sit down to write many paths appear before me to entice me to follow and today is no exception. I am remembering a morning so long ago as I stood in my kitchen washing my morning dishes. My children, who were only young at the time, were playing in the next room close by and my husband had been called out to attend to work. As I moved from the sink area to pick up a saucepan from my stove close by, I became aware of something happening before my eyes. I could not make it out or even imagine what had just happened so I continued on to pick up the item from the stove - what followed next was something I could not have stopped seeing, even if I had wanted to for my eyes were wide open.

As I looked I could see the top of a man's head for it appeared I was looking down upon him.

He was naked and visible to his waist and his arms were extended and visible to about his elbows. I knew instantly who it represented and as I looked, the man turned his head and rolled it to the other side where it rested. It was not like seeing someone on the television or a movie screen it was like the person was in the room with me and I knew it was the Lord Jesus Christ on the Cross, yet he did not have a mark on him there were no crown of thorns nor physical marks or blood upon him, he was perfect and I knew it was the Lord. Recognizing my Savior I immediately said, Oh everything I have been taught was truth.

Then a feeling of great sorrow came over me and somewhere deep within me, whelmed up a huge tear which then fell from my eye.

As I recall this vision today, I believe I understand why I was allowed to see my savior the Lord Jesus Christ upon that cross as I did that day, and the consolation that it has given me when I realized you can be crucified by others, and not have one mark upon your person to show that it is happening.

Along with the memory of that wonderful vision, the thing that comes back to me is the thought of that huge tear that came from my eye, as I recognized its shape of that of a rugby football.

Thank you Father God for your great mercy in showing me your beloved son that day, for it has been a blessing that no one can take away from me and makes me all the more determined to tell you daily how much I believe in you. Knowing you and your Holy Word is truth and it brings great joy and hope for all who seek you.

Yes, my Lord Jesus Christ, Yes, I believe in all that you and your Father and the Holy Spirit have allowed me to receive in my life. Yes, I want to thank you for my husband and family who have stood with me, not knowing at times where I was coming from. Amen.

My Prayer

My Lord and my God, how I seek to do your will in order to honor you and praise you in Jesus Holy Name. Amen.

Words Received

There will be a new beginning Pam, for you and for all people who turn away from their sins and repent and come follow me. The sun has shone for a long time upon the earth, giving its warmth to enable it to continue to bring about growth for all who live upon it. Yet many people never gave a thought to how that sun obeyed me. Scientists made their own observations and set down their conclusions and decided that they knew all about it. Then one day the sun decided to make its presence felt, and only then did man decide to look up to see what was happening.

Today from your television, you see fire burning up the country side, destroying everything in its path - no one escapes its force without exerting much pressure.

You like many others have wondered what will become of planet earth, had you read my Holy Word carefully you would realise that the earth and all that is in it belongs to me. All people who have tried to own or destroy it in the effort to own it and control it will not succeed for long. My hand will always be ready to bring down the tyrant and expose the stealer.

Are you able to write these words for your book? If so, remember there are still people who love me and who know that I am God and like you, they will be encouraged to hear my words; claiming that I will do what must be done to restore my planet earth to its full beauty.

People first must realise that I alone am the all-knowing and when men and women start to believe that their own knowledge will save them, then and only then, will they realise that there will always be one more thing needed to support the knowledge that they think they possess.

Angels have gathered here in this land and they too watch as it burns for they have been sent to ease the suffering of the poor, not to interfere with the work of the evil one, for He has to have his time to sift my people. If he succeeds, that will be such a shame for them for they will not know what they have lost. He will be allotted time for such an action and no person will be excluded from that sifting.

Pam, when the time comes for him to be revealed there will be much snarling and gnashing of teeth from those who have been caught in his snare. So many people have put away faith to follow worldly pursuits. They believe that popularity and sporting achievements will be what they need to complete their lives and to bring them success and prosperity.

Have I not told you through my Holy Word, that it is better to sit at your own table in humble surroundings, than to sit at the table of kings and queens and others in high places, where you have to watch what and how you eat because if you do not agree with them you will be cast outside never to return again. Knowing the stress it causes you, your own health may suffer.

Be happy and contented with what you have, on and at your own table. When you invite someone to eat with you, do it for the right reason and not to seek something for yourself in return.

Politicians live two lives which is such a shame, the one they portray in the direction of the public and the one they love behind closed doors. Mighty men and women have fallen into the trough that waits just inside these doors where many enter in good faith, but over time become complacent and began to eat from the forbidden fruits laid out before them. Hold high the person you find who is faithful and true for they are worthy of being honored in your midst.

Why have I asked you to write this - this day?

Why Pam, many have already said what I am telling you - but in many cases no one will listen. Maybe, just maybe, if those who say they love and follow me hear that I am also saying these things they may be able to stop from being deceived by the enemy and just stop and back away from his path of darkness.

My Prayer

My Lord, I have had a request from someone to contact a certain person this morning, but somehow I don't feel like opening up my heart again just to accommodate them today. Please have mercy on me for the way I am feeling. So hard not to just shut down - what should I do? Please don't abandon me in this position, for I don't know that I can cope anymore.

Words Received

Believe my daughter, just believe, I am coming with help, with healing and with peace and joy to fill the spaces that have been torn apart in your life. Shine for me, just remember they have had their time and now they must enter into that place where you have been.

It will not be nice for them either, for they failed to show mercy towards you. You did not understand, but what I wanted from you I could not ask of them. My hand will bring about a new understanding for yourself and your loved ones.

Go in peace.

My Prayer

Dear Lord, I am sorry about not writing I hope you understand. I really do want to be obedient to you, but I sometimes get lost. I come today to do your will before anything else. In Jesus Name I make this prayer. Amen

Words Received

Believing is such a blessing Pam, for you believed this day that what I had asked you to do, that being listening and writing, you have remembered to do. So child I am indeed pleased, so let us begin.

The story that you spoke about in your book is truly a story of interest too and for many. You see they have become

like lost sheep and each of the mob of sheep have been wandering into fields that are not theirs. Just like sheep, people also have wandered away into areas they should not have ventured into. I am calling my sheep, those who know my voice, to return to their rightful place. My sheep know my voice and I tell them to hurry quickly to that safe place where there will be protection for them against the snares of the enemy.

Child why do you believe so many became so lost. Do you imagine that their intelligence was the cause of it- or- do you, like some, understand that it is when people no longer show respect for anything or anyone?

My heavenly beings are watching in amazement at the antics of some and are wondering how long it will be before I give them the order to commence their duty to bring quickly order back to the people of the earth. I did it before and I will do it again, if I need to.

Show yourself by putting together these words and let it be read. Some will believe and others will not but you will have done as I asked. Go in peace. Amen.

Monday 23rd March 2020

My Prayer

Dear Lord as the Coronavirus pandemic continues on around the world, I see we the people becoming more separated by law in order to keep the virus from spreading.

As I awoke this morning my first thoughts were in prayer to you and after prayer I remembered some of the things you had told me in the past, some things I was told a little before the bush fires and other things after the fires here in Australia. Remembering each disaster that hovered over our land and indeed the whole world, I especially remember where I spoke to you about my reaction to the same sex marriage bill that was made into law and the pride of the people on that day. Adam and Eve turned away from your holy word and did not listen; they were driven out of your garden and were made to keep themselves alive by the sweat of their brow.

When I spoke to you about this, I believed it was not only about the yes vote becoming law - it was the feeling that we and this land, Australia would be given our own wakeup call after it happened. I also felt at the time that whatever was to come would be out of our control.

Since that time I have watched as the country in some places still struggle with drought, other parts have suffered destruction with weather patterns causing severe hailstorms and utility service outages. This morning I wake to the COVID 19 latest warnings to the people to try and keep them safe – with the closures of places where people may gather in groups, such as clubs, pubs, cinemas, sporting events and even your Holy House has had to close its doors.

Yet, I see so many young and not so young continuing to want to live as if they are here only for a good time, not for a long time. Having said that, I somehow feel if they were to catch this virus and their life was in danger, they would really want someone to help them survive.

Well Father, having listened to the latest warnings coming from our Government Leaders, I was so happy to remember the day I spoke to you about our wakeup call and the many times I had come across that word *change*, for we are now being told that we all must change to fight this virus and we must obey the rules of the law.

Again I have taken comfort from the words I received after speaking to you about our wakeup call and what that could mean.

The words I received that day were:

Go in peace Pam you have foreseen the future this night - but be not afraid for the enemy of the Lord is not in control as many may think. He has been allowed to menace for some time but the battle he has been waging will come to naught.

Lord, the above has all been my thoughts for today with the exception of the words I received at the end of my writing. I am wondering if there is anything you want me to listen to and write today. In Jesus mighty name I make this prayer. Amen.

Words Received

Believe my child, for all I have told you has come from My Father; it would be beneficial to all people for you to print this book quickly and allow it to be circulated wherever. Go in peace and do your best to bring this about.

Today is 23rd March 2020, and having received the above words, I will try and be obedient to what has been asked of me.

18.
CLOSING IN OBEDIENCE

I humbly call upon the one who has great persuasion with our Divine Savior Our Lord Jesus Christ, that one being His Blessed Mother, and I seek her intercession for the protection of our country Australia and for the whole world at this time.

Some time back I started writing about remembering an old movie I had seen in which the Blessed Virgin Mary was a prominent character in the story.

Now, I feel it is time to close my thoughts for this book, by sharing something that was not a movie but something very real. I am remembering a cold and wintery Sunday night in the church in Goulburn where my son and I were attending Mass - he was a young teenager at the time rugged up in his heavy coat for warmth against the cold.

A young priest was saying the Mass and on giving his sermon he spoke much about our lady. When it came time to go to Holy Communion my son and I got up from our seat in the back part of the church where there where very few people. As we entered the aisle of the church there was no one near us, but all of a sudden this wonderful perfume surrounded us and we both looked at each other, not knowing where the beautiful perfume came from for, we were the only two people in that part of the church at the time.

To this day some thirty years later we still remember and talk about this moment when Our Lady's perfume permeated our part of the church after the priest had so lovingly talked about our Lady in his sermon.

Closing my thoughts with these last few words, I humbly ask the Blessed Virgin Mary to intercede for us and the world with her Divine Son for mercy. Mother Mary we are all sinners and have wandered away like sheep into different pastures and places where we were not meant to go. This has caused many to become confused by all the different voices, choices, and opinions being offered to them and who after time, decide upon the most appropriate voice that suited them best to follow.

Oh Mary, as a Mother we are in desperate need of a Mothers love and intercession at this time, for many have failed to heed the warning and have failed in honoring your Divine Son the Lord Jesus Christ. Now, the Fathers hand has been laid upon us and we are like sheep without our shepherd.

Please Mother Mary, intercede with God the Father for mercy, for we have in many cases, not honored Him (God the Son) as we should - and have brought him down to man's level by failing to remember, HE is GOD THE SON - THE SECOND PERSON OF THE BLESSED TRINITY.

The Father is God

The Son is God and

The Holy Spirit is God

There are Three Persons but there is only One God.

May the God of the Trinity be praised and glorified forever.

Amen.